Vapour Trails
And Other Stories

by

Roy Porter

Grosvenor House
Publishing Limited

This book is published by
Grosvenor House Publishing Ltd
Link House
140 The Broadway, Tolworth, Surrey, KT6 7HT.
www.grosvenorhousepublishing.co.uk

This book is a work of fiction. Any resemblance to
people or events, past or present, is purely coincidental.

A CIP record for this book
is available from the British Library

ISBN 978-1-83975-137-0

Vapour Trails in the Sky

CHAPTER 1

Anne Lyndsay watched with sad eyes as the jet plane's vapour trails streaked across the azure blue sky. She couldn't be sure if it was that exact plane, but she knew her friend Irene Blair had recently headed off on a flight to Australia. The two women had been friends since childhood, and 23 years ago Irene had walked behind Anne on her wedding day.

Irene had never married; she was too much of a career girl. She had lived with her sister Pearl in their late parents' home, until Pearl met and married Ken Jones, an Australian businessman who convinced her to move back to his native country to live. Sadly, five years after they moved to settle in Perth, Ken succumbed to a heart attack and died.

With their only child, Robert, still at college in Perth, Pearl never considered coming home to the UK. And she had made plenty of friends in the city, and their companionship helped her through her grief. However, Irene became increasingly unsettled, and within two years of Ken's death, she decided to emigrate.

On the death of both their parents, the house had been bequeathed to the two sisters or, if one died, to the remaining sister. And when Irene told Pearl of her decision to move to Australia, the sisters agreed it would be best to rent the house out fully furnished through an estate agent friend of Irene's.

Naturally, Pearl was delighted that her sister had decided to move closer to her, but Anne was sad to see her friend go. She understood, however, that as the saying goes, blood is thicker than water.

Anne knew Irene had stayed overnight with a former work-mate in Solihull, so that she could easily catch a flight from Birmingham to Perth, with a brief stopover in Qatar.

Irene had given Anne the Solihull telephone number, and the two friends had enjoyed a final chat before Anne wished her a good journey and Irene promised to telephone when she got to Australia.

Heading back into the house, Anne opened the photo drawer and began looking through her old albums. Another shadow crossed her mind as she looked at her wedding pictures. Her husband William had suffered a second stroke in October 2011 and died within two weeks. In many ways, it had been a blessing, as Anne knew that he could not have coped with being paralysed. The pair had not enjoyed the pleasure of parenthood and had considered adoption, but when William's health began to deteriorate, they had both known it wasn't an option.

Closing her eyes, Anne replayed memories of growing up with Irene, chuckling as she remembered some of her school-friend's antics, including one occasion when she had accepted a dare to climb over the playground wall into the headmaster's garden to retrieve a boy's football. Their years at Clooney Primary School had been good ones, as both had been clever pupils, passing their 11+ with high grades. She smiled as she remembered their years at Foyle College, social evenings at their church, choosing partners for the College 'Formal', and the occasional visit to the local dance hall with dates but no long-term relationships.

The two friends had headed off to university – Anne to Queens to study nursing; Irene to Bristol, where she studied law. Irene had gone on to be a very successful solicitor in Londonderry, while Anne had nursed first in The Royal Victoria Hospital, Belfast, and later in Altnagelvin Hospital in her home city, where she met William.

She had laughingly accepted his telephone number, knowing that patients often form a crush on their nurses. But to her surprise, within two weeks of his discharge, she'd received a phone call from William. Apparently, one of her cheeky colleagues had, with a wink, slipped him her phone number as he left the ward.

They dated, fell in love, and within two years were married. If anything, though, these precious memories only increased Anne's feelings of loneliness and despair. Her husband had gone, and now her childhood friend had left, although Anne didn't begrudge Irene her new life.

She sighed heavily. 'I'll put the kettle on,' she said to Wendy, her tabby cat. Putting her memories safely back in the drawer, she headed for the kitchen.

The following morning, Anne switched the radio on to listen to the news as she sat down to eat breakfast.

'...and now some breaking news,' the announcer said. 'A plane which flew from Birmingham Airport, bound for Perth, Australia, is believed to have crashed just off the coast of Spain. The captain of a fishing vessel witnessed the plane nose-dive into the sea. He reported seeing flames from the rear of the plane. The Boeing 767 had 260 passengers on board. Initial reports suggest that there were no survivors. We will bring you further details in our next news bulletin.'

Anne froze, her teacup inches away from her lips, then with a strangled cry she replaced her cup on its saucer and reach-ed for a pen to jot down the emergency number which the announcer read out. Her hands shaking and here heart thump-ing, she dialled the number several times without success, each time receiving a busy signal.

'Oh, what shall I do? What shall I do?' Anne cried out in anguish. She looked up the number for Birmingham Airport and tried that, but it too was busy.

'Sorry, your call cannot be answered at this time,' was the automated message.

As the morning dragged on, she watched the BBC News channel hoping for further information, but with nothing new to report the announcer repeated the telephone helpline number. Once again, Anne tried the airport emergency number, and this time someone answered.

After she explained that the passenger she was concerned about had no family in the UK, the operator took Irene's name and Anne's telephone number, and assured her that she would be treated as a family member and would receive information as soon as it became available.

The evening news had information about the search teams recovering more pieces of wreckage, but no evidence of survivors. Exhausted, Anne decided to have an early night and went through her bedtime routine before climbing into bed with a heavy heart.

* * * * * *

Surprisingly, Anne slept well and it was the telephone, not the alarm, which wakened her. She glanced at her bedside clock – 7.30am – then lifted the phone.

Expecting to hear from the helpline, she was surprised to hear an Australian accent; the caller had a young male voice.

'Hello,' he said, 'is that my Aunt Irene's friend, Anne?'

'It is,' she replied.

'Hi, this is Robert and my mum Pearl is concerned that on the news it said that investigations were ongoing regarding a plane crash off the coast of Spain. A search found pieces of wreckage they said, but no survivors. Aunt Irene said she would ring when her flight landed in Qatar, but she didn't. Oh, here's my mum.'

'Hi Anne,' said Pearl. 'Robert and I drove to the airport, but her flight wasn't listed. We queued with others at the information desk, only to be informed that if we left our names and addresses and the name of the plane passengers, the airport would get in touch as soon as possible. Some decided to wait at the airport for news, but we decided to come home and ring you. Do you know anything about a plane crash?'

'Not yet,' Anne replied. 'But I am awaiting information from the airport. As soon as I know anything, I'll let you know. Let me write down your number.'

'I'll text it to you,' Pearl responded. 'What's your mobile number?'

'Ah,' replied Anne, 'I'm not mobile or computer literate.' She heard Pearl sigh as she wrote down the number.

'Ok, thanks,' Anne also sighed. 'Bye.'

A few minutes later, the phone rang again. 'Hello, Mrs Lyndsay?' the caller asked.

'That's me,' Anne replied.

The caller continued, 'This is the helpline at Birmingham Airport. I have some interesting news for you. Your friend, Mrs Irene Blair, checked in but didn't board the plane. Several calls were made, but she didn't respond so her luggage was removed and placed in the Left Luggage Office. We have no information regarding her whereabouts, but the good news is that she was not on board the plane that crashed.'

Anne thanked the caller and replaced the phone on its cradle. Her mind whirling, she immediately dialled the number Pearl had provided.

'Hi, it's Anne. I have news,' she said when Pearl answered. 'It seems Irene checked in at the airport but did not board the plane.'

After a pause to let this sink in, Pearl asked, 'Why? What can we do now?'

'First,' replied Anne, 'I am going to have my breakfast then I'll get a flight to Birmingham Airport to collect her luggage. I'll ask some questions when I get there, and see what I can find out.'

Anne asked her neighbour, Miss Tomkins, if she would look after Wendy, then drove to the Belfast International Airport where she checked her car into the long stay car park and dashed off to catch the first available flight to Birmingham.

CHAPTER 2

Anne had flown into Birmingham on numerous occasions during her working life. As a nurse, she had often accompanied patients needing specialised treatment at Birmingham General Hospital.

Those were great times, Anne thought to herself, as she pondered for a while on her days as a nurse.

She had nursed her husband William when, as a relatively young man, he had suffered heart problems – atrial fibrillation. Eventually, he'd had a pacemaker fitted which helped, and in later life this had been removed and replaced with an ICD, an implantable cardioverter defibrillator. Only on one occasion had the device delivered an electric shock when the pacemaker part did not control his heart rhythms. It hadn't been a pleasant experience but his life had been saved and the only down side had been that he was not allowed to drive for six weeks. By that time, William had retired from his engineering job and spent most of his day in the garden, with occasional cruise holidays with Anne, mainly to the Mediterranean.

Now back in Birmingham for the first time in years, Anne found the information desk and made enquiries about Irene. The staff could tell her very little other than to confirm that she had checked in but hadn't then boarded the ill-fated plane.

Anne had permission to collect Irene's two cases from the Left Luggage, but decided to make some more enquiries first. Realising that it was time to get technical, she headed to the airport's Vodafone shop, where she explained her circumstances and asked for help. The assistant produced an inexpensive little mobile phone that, he told her, could do all she required.

Taking her address book from her handbag, Anne asked if he could install some numbers and show her how to access them.

'Come with me,' he said, and took her into a rear office. Another assistant, a girl, appeared and asked if she would like tea or coffee.

'Oh, tea would be lovely,' Anne replied.

The male assistant, whose name tag read Charlie, began the instruction process. After tea and two Rich Tea biscuits, Anne experimented by calling Pearl. She explained where she was and now 'mobilised', then gave Pearl her number and assured her she would keep in touch.

Anne had also made a note of the number of Irene's friend in Solihull and rang her.

'Hello,' she said, 'my name is Anne Lyndsay, Irene's friend.'

'Oh yes, Irene rang you from here,' the caller replied. 'I'm Jayne Thorpe, by the way. Have you heard from Irene?'

'No,' replied Anne, 'that's why I'm ringing. The plane she was to travel on crashed, but as it transpired, she wasn't on it. Her luggage is at the airport, but she has disappeared.'

'Oh, my word!' Jayne exclaimed. 'Keith, my husband, and I were on a coach trip to London with an overnight stay. We've only just returned. Are you at home?'

'No,' Anne explained, 'I've come over to Birmingham Airport to try and get some information.'

'Right, then why don't I come and collect you and you can stay here until you decide what to do. We'd love to help in any way.'

'Thank you,' Anne said in response to the invitation, 'and your help would be invaluable.'

'Okay then,' Jayne continued. 'Stay in the airport and collect Irene's luggage. I'll park and meet you. Look out for a lady in a red coat and black beret, that'll be me.'

Anne sat in the café area with a good view of the entrance doors and drank a cup of tea, accompanied by a digestive biscuit. She had just risen from her table when she spotted a lady dressed in the way Jayne had described. Anne waved to her as she walked towards the entrance, and the woman waved back.

As they collected the luggage, Anne suddenly had an idea. 'There wasn't a handbag handed is was there?' she asked the assistant.

'Oh,' the friendly young woman responded, 'you probably mean the one belonging to the lady who had the accident on the escalator.'

'Perhaps,' said Anne. 'What happened to her?'

Pointing, the assistant explained, 'It was on that escalator over there. I think it may have been the gentleman's fault. He was ahead of her then they both came tumbling down. I watched as the medics checked them over and then carried them out on stretchers. A little while later, a cleaner found a handbag under the escalator and handed it in. I'll get it and you can check if it belongs to your friend.'

A short time later, she came back with the handbag. 'What did you say your friend was called?'

'Irene Blair,' replied Jayne.

The assistant drew a passport out of the bag, checked the details, then showed the photo to Jayne and Anne.

Anne answered, 'Yes, that is Irene, and her address is 14 Shepherd's Way, Waterside, Londonderry.'

The assistant checked the passport again. 'Ok, if you sign a release document, you can have the bag.'

'I'll let Anne do that,' said Jayne. 'She was her lifelong friend and neighbour.'

With the form signed and the bag in Anne's possession, the two women made their way to the nearest coffee shop.

'She will most likely have been admitted to the main Birmingham Hospital,' said Jayne, 'so we'll check there first.'

As they sipped their hot drinks, Anne could only watch in amazement as Jayne typed information into her mobile phone, then scribbled a telephone number on the table napkin, then repeated this a few more times, scribbling noting down several more numbers.

'Right,' Jayne said eventually, 'we'll start with Birmingham City.'

With that, she tapped a number into her phone. 'Hello,' she said and asked for admissions. When she got through, Jayne asked if a Mrs Irene Blair had been admitted to A&E on the 13th, following an accident at the airport.

'I have no record of anyone named Irene Blair having been admitted on that date,' the receptionist from admissions replied. 'But there was a gentleman and a lady admitted from the airport. We had a name for the man but not for the lady.' She paused briefly. 'I see they are both in Ward 7; let me put you through.'

'Hello, Ward 7, Sister Graham speaking, how can I help you?' said another voice.

Again, Jayne explained the reason for their call and suggested the female patient's name might be Irene Blair.

After a brief pause, Sister Graham said, 'The lady who came in after the airport accident had no identification, and I'm afraid she is in a coma. We informed the police, who were to ask at the airport. However, if you would like to come to the ward, I will let you see her and possibly make an identification.'

'Thank you,' Jayne responded. 'We're at the airport right now, but we will be with you shortly.'

Jayne and Anne finished their drinks then headed to Jayne's car, where Anne insisted on paying the parking fee.

CHAPTER 3

The journey to the hospital took three-quarters of an hour, and Jayne managed to find a space in the multi-storey car park. Once inside the hospital, the two women took the lift to Ward 7 where they met Sister Graham. Anne showed Irene's passport photo to her, and the senior nurse nodded. 'Yes, that does look like our patient. Come with me.'

They were led to a side room off the ward where they found Irene lying on a bed, her head encased in some sort of protective cage, and a battery of equipment monitoring her condition.

'Yes,' whispered Anne, 'that is my friend, Irene Blair. What's the prognosis?'

'We are not sure,' the sister replied. 'There is some bruising to the top of the spine, and the x-rays showed a skull fracture, hence the head protection as Doctor Emery doesn't want her waking up and making any sudden movements. Brain damage hasn't been ruled out, so he has arranged for an MRI scan. The scan is scheduled for this afternoon at two o'clock.'

'Irene and I grew up together, and she is my best friend,' Anne informed Sister Graham. 'Her only relative is in Australia, so I would like to remain here until the scan result comes through and decisions have to be made.'

'That's no problem,' the sister assured her. 'Stay as long as you wish. It might be a good idea to talk to her.' She smiled reassuringly. 'Who can tell? It might have a positive effect.'

When the sister left the room, Anne and Jayne pulled up chairs next to Irene's bed and started chatting to her. To their surprise, a tray of tea and biscuits appeared a few minutes later, brought in by a nurse.

'Oh, thank you,' Anne and Irene both responded.

'You're welcome,' said the nurse, who smiled and left.

'Well, now that we have found her,' said Jayne, 'I'll finish this tea then leave Irene in your capable hands. I need to get back home and unpack. You've got my number, so ring me later on, and I will come and get you. Although we solved our mystery much quicker than we thought, you are still welcome to stay with us.'

Anne shook her head. 'Unfortunately, you live in Solihull,' she said, 'and I could not impose on you daily, not knowing how long this will go on. No, I will book into a nearby hotel for a few nights, and they decide what's best to do.'

She rose and gave Jayne a hug. 'Thank you for your help today, and don't worry, I will keep you updated.'

'Ok,' Jayne responded, 'but I will come in again. Maybe not tomorrow because I have other plans, but Saturday definitely.' Another hug and Jayne was gone.

Anne walked out to the ward reception, where she found the friendly young nurse who had brought the tea.

'Hello,' said Anne, 'I am planning to stay for a few days and wonder, could you suggest a hotel or guest house within walking distance of the hospital?'

'Why yes, of course,' the nurse replied. 'I would suggest the Sherwood Hotel. It is quite close, and I believe very comfortable. I have friends who stayed there last year.'

'Thank you,' Anne replied. 'I'll go there now, but I'll leave you my mobile number so please ring me if there is any change. I will be in again 'As the scan results probably won't be back until the morning, I'll come back then.'

With that Anne wrote her number on the nurse's proffered pad and left to find the Sherwood Hotel, and to make a call to Australia to give Pearl the news.

After a night in a very comfortable bed and a delicious breakfast, Anne made her way through the early shoppers to the hospital where she received a report on Irene; there was no change in her condition. Anne felt quite teary-eyed as she looked down at her friend.

Suddenly, Irene's eyelids flickered and her eyes opened. Anne quietly spoke her friend's name and at the same time pressed the buzzer. A nurse entered the room.

'Her eyes opened briefly,' said Anne.

The nurse leaned over, and spoke to Irene but there was no response.

'Irene, your friend Anne is here,' she tried again. 'Would you like to see her?'

Still no response. 'I'll contact the doctor,' said the nurse.

After a few minutes, the doctor and the ward sister arrived.

'Go down to the common room at the end of the corridor,' advised the sister, 'and I'll have someone bring you a cuppa. I'll ask the doctor to speak to you there.'

As Anne sat in the small room with her tea and biscuits, she listened to the busyness in the corridor. Her mind drifted back to her own nursing days when things had been just as busy but less technical and a lot less paperwork. She wondered where her colleagues of those days were now. *I suppose married and retired, just like me.*

Anne had just finished her tea when the door opened, and the doctor entered. He shook Anne's hand. 'I'm Doctor Emery,' he said, 'and you are, I believe, a close friend.'

'Yes,' replied Anne. 'Irene, her sister Pearl and I grew up together.'

'Well,' continued the doctor, 'the scan shows slight brain damage, sort of bruising. She is showing signs of agitation so I feel it would be better to put her into an induced coma and we will keep her under 24-hour observation. I assure you a nurse will be present at all times. I wouldn't want anyone present for the time being, so if we have your contact details we can keep you updated.'

'How long will she be in the coma?' Anne asked.

'That is hard to tell,' the doctor replied. 'But be assured, we will contact you when we have any news.'

'Thank you,' said Anne, 'I will update her sister in Australia, but meanwhile I need to arrange to fly home. You can reach me there, so I'll leave my home number as well.'

* * * * * *

Before leaving the hospital, Anne made two phone calls. One to Pearl in Australia, updating her on her sister's condition and treatment; it wasn't an easy conversation. The second call was to Jayne, giving her an update and explaining that the doctor advised no visitors for a few days. Anne also told her she planned to go home.

Jayne reminded Anne that Irene's luggage was still in the boot of her car, and suggested that she look after until such times as the hospital determined Irene's future.

'I will phone the hospital,' Jayne continued, 'and I'll visit when permitted.' She then wished Anne a safe trip and said goodbye.

Anne walked back to her hotel, where she asked the receptionist if could check for flights to Belfast.

'Of course,' the helpful young woman replied. 'I will do it right now.'

After checking flight times, the receptionist wrote them down and gave the paper to Anne.

'You can book your flight at the airport,' she said, 'but you would be advised to get there about an hour and a half to book and check-in. Would you like me to make out your bill?'

'Yes, please,' replied Anne. 'I'll go and get my case. And would you phone for a taxi to the airport?'

'No problem,' the receptionist responded.

A few minutes later Anne checked out, and was in the taxi to the airport.

She had no bother booking an early flight, and within two-and-a-half hours of leaving the hotel, she was airborne.

After the short flight, Anne paid the parking fee, collected her car and headed for Londonderry and home. She thanked Miss Wilkins for looking after her cat, and curled up with Wendy on the settee and slept.

CHAPTER 4

In the charity shop where Anne worked part-time, her colleagues welcomed her back and wanted to know how her trip went. She told them her news regarding the flights, the hospital visit, her overnight stay, and the continued anxious wait for news.

When she got home, there were two messages on her phone answering machine. The first was from Pearl to say that she and Robert had decided to fly to Birmingham and stay close to Irene. She also enquired about the hotel where Anne had stayed. The second call was from Jayne, just to say she would phone later and hoped Anne had arrived home safely.

Anne looked at her watch; it was too late to phone Pearl. She turned on her oven and placed a cottage pie-for-one inside and set her timer.

Whilst waiting for her dinner to cook, she turned on the television to watch the evening news. There was no mention of the plane crash and Anne marvelled at how swiftly news faded into oblivion. When the oven timer pinged, she opened a small tin of beans and emptied the contents into a bowl which she heated in the microwave. Within minutes her dinner was complete; a meal she enjoyed with a drink of blackcurrant juice.

Afterwards, Anne settled down to watch the evening television programmes, but there was nothing new on the plane crash.

* * * * * *

Pearl had explained the situation to Robert's college headmaster, and compassionate leave was granted. But he would have to study via the college's teaching website. Pearl's neighbour, Bob, assured her he would keep a regular check on her house, so she gave him a key.

Anne had phoned with details about the Sherwood Hotel, and before leaving home, Pearl had rung and booked an indefinite stay. She gave the hotel her credit card number, after being assured of tight security.

Pearl and Robert flew out on Thursday evening, the 23rd of May, first to Dubai then, after a five-hour stopover, their plane headed for Birmingham.

Once settled into their hotel, Pearl suddenly felt the results of the jet lag, as did Robert. She wanted to be fresh before visiting her sister, so she and her son lay on top of their beds and, covered with the available blankets, slept.

Back in Londonderry, Anne received a phone call from Birmingham City Hospital to say that Irene had wakened from her coma and was sitting up eating. Anne was asked to come into the hospital to talk with the administrator.

Anne explained that she was now back in Londonderry, but that Irene's sister Pearl Jones had flown from Australia and was staying at the Sherwood Hotel. She suggested that the hospital should contact Pearl there.

Later that evening, Anne had a phone call from Pearl.

'She is sitting up and very alert, but paralysed from the waist down. The damage to her spinal cord is quite severe...' her voice broke slightly before she went on, 'and the chances are Irene may never walk again. But the doctor said, "never say never", so I am hopeful.'

'That is good news regarding her initial recovery,' Anne told her. 'So, what are your immediate plans?'

Pearl informed Anne that there would be several weeks of physiotherapy before Irene could leave hospital, and that she had contacted friends back home regarding Robert.

'I feel it is best that Robert returns to continue his studies,' Pearl continued, 'and he will stay with my friend Beth and her husband Tony. Their son Gareth is at college with Robert, so that will work out fine. I will stay here, but once Irene is able to leave hospital, I intend to take her back with me to Perth. When he gets back home, I'll get Robert to go to our house and find the contact details for the agent who is looking after our Derry home.'

'No need to do that,' Anne interrupted. 'Irene gave me his address and number before heading off. Hold on and I will get the information.'

She quickly found the required address and telephone number, and relayed the information to Pearl.

'I've made an executive decision to sell the house,' said Pearl, 'so I will contact our solicitor, he's a cousin, and he can take care of all the formalities.' She thanked Anne for her help and asked what had happened to Irene's luggage.

'It is with her friend, Jayne,' Anne assured her. 'Let me contact her and have her call you. Or, if you can ask Irene to call and update her, I am sure Jayne would like to hear from you both.'

'Yes, I know Jayne,' said Pearl, 'and I will talk to Irene later at the hospital. Once again, thank you for all you have done. I'll keep in touch and let you know how things work out.'

* * * * * *

Three weeks and numerous phone calls later, an uneasy Anne decided to return to Birmingham and talk to Irene face-to-face. Once again, she took the short flight and booked into the Sherwood Hotel. At breakfast, a surprised Pearl stopped in amazement as she entered the dining room and was greeted by a smiling Anne.

'I couldn't stay away any longer,' Anne explained, as Pearl and Robert joined at her table. 'I wanted to see Irene for myself.'

'What a lovely surprise to see you face-to-face and not voice-to-voice on the telephone,' laughed Pearl.

Robert had not spoken until the ladies had finished their greetings. 'Hello, Mrs Lyndsay,' he said eventually.

'Oh no,' Anne responded. 'Please call me Anne; Mrs Lyndsay is so formal.'

With breakfast over, all three walked to the hospital. The October morning was warm and bright, and they enjoyed their walk in the autumn sunshine. Anne asked about life in Australia, and both Pearl and Robert responded enthusiastically.

In the hospital ward, Irene's face lit up when she saw Anne, and they greeted each other affectionately. Her friend's spirits were high, in spite of her future prospects.

'I suppose, from now on, football with Robert is out of the question,' she quirked smiling at Robert and taking his hand.

'We can always play basketball,' he retorted, laughing.

The doctor's round ended their chat, and Anne kissed Irene and Pearl goodbye. Robert drew back in horror as she leaned towards him.

'We'll keep our goodbyes formal, Mrs Lyndsay,' he said, holding up his hands with a laugh.

'I am going back on the morning flight,' Anne explained to Irene. 'But I just had to see you. Get well, and every blessing for the future.'

Robert kissed his aunt goodbye. 'I am also flying home tomorrow, but I look forward to seeing you in Australia soon.'

In the hospital entrance hall, they met Jayne and her husband, Keith.

'The hotel receptionist told us we would find you here,' said Jayne, after Anne made the introductions. 'I brought Irene's luggage. I left it at the hotel for you.'

'Let us take you on a tour of our city and then out to lunch,' suggested Keith. 'I know a lovely restaurant. I am sure your hotel food is good, but the food at this restaurant is great'.

After an interesting city tour in Keith's people carrier, they enjoyed a scrumptious meal at Keith's suggested restaurant before returning to the Sherwood Hotel. Robert played on the pool table while Anne and Pearl went to their rooms for a much-needed afternoon nap.

CHAPTER 5

Anne, still full from her lunch, decided to forgo dinner. She rang Pearl's room and explained that she wasn't at all hungry but would perhaps join Pearl and Robert in the lounge for coffee afterwards. Pearl had also decided to skip dinner, but, even after his big lunch, Robert wanted to eat.

'I'll join you now in the lounge if you like,' she offered, 'and we can chat while Robert eats.'

Robert joined them for coffee, and they discussed the future.

'Once she can fly, Irene will come to Australia with me,' Pearl informed Anne. 'I belong to a fine medical practice, and I'm sure the doctors there will look after Irene.'

Once again, goodbyes were said, and Anne wished Robert a safe flight. She knew Pearl and Robert were leaving early for the airport, and she would have checked out by the time Pearl returned to the hotel. It was unlikely they would bump into one another at the airport.

The next morning, after her flight and car journey home, Anne once again thanked her neighbour for keeping an eye on Wendy. She suddenly felt exhausted.

* * * * * *

On the morning news, radio listeners heard that divers had found the wreckage of the plane which had crashed just off the coast of Spain. They found the bodies of the pilot and co-pilot, and reported that the plane had split into two; some passengers were visible in the tail section. The divers could see no passengers in the front section, which had sustained the most damage, possibly caused by crashing on the rocky ocean floor. Plans were underway to recover the flight's black box recorder and, hopefully, the bodies of those still on board.

* * * * * *

Following several weeks of medical care and physio, Irene was discharged and pronounced fit to fly. Pearl, who was now lodging with Jayne and had given Anne regular updates, called again with the news.

She and Irene, with an appropriate insurance premium organised, flew out from Birmingham City Airport on the long journey to Perth. For Pearl, it was a journey to Robert and home; for Irene, a new life and a new lifestyle – though not the one she had originally envisaged. For Anne, it was back to the routine of housework, charity work, and Wendy care.

However, any time vapour trails appeared in the sky above Londonderry, Anne would whisper a prayer of thanks for Irene's safety, but sigh at the loss of a lifetime friend.

Jake and The Jersey Girl

CHAPTER 1

Lisa Craig had never been to Jersey before, so when her friend Erin Pearce – born on the island – suggested a holiday there, she agreed... but with little enthusiasm. Lisa was a person of habit, and that included holiday destinations. Although Lisa was 22 years old, she still lived at home with her parents, Bill and Alice, and her much younger brother, 14-year-old Leslie. Her idea of a holiday was a week in the sun with a good book. Or a caravan trip with the family, usually to Cornwall.

Erin, on the other hand, was a traveller. Her father James Pearce, a Jersey-born British soldier, was based in Germany. As a child, Erin had travelled with her dad and mum, Grace, to army bases in Cyprus, the Middle East, and following the troubles in Northern Ireland, to Palace Barracks, Holywood, where her two brothers, Joseph and Kyle, were born. Following his demob, her father had accepted a position with his brother Eric, who had a removal and storage facility in Stevenage, Kent. Eric had left Jersey in his early twenties.

* * * * * *

Eric's job as a long-distance lorry driver had taken him to the UK on several occasions and, during one trip, he met Gary White, an ex-long-distance driver. He and Gary had previously met several times at lunch stopovers on the London to Birmingham route, and Gary had shared his dream of one day owning a trucking company. They had laughed and joked about a partnership in this dream company, and exchanged letters for a time, still dreaming.

Tragedy struck when, on holiday in France, a landslide occurred in the Mercantour National Park. Three cars, including Eric's, were swept into a valley. He survived, but spent six months in hospital where surgeons carried out several operations on his badly damaged legs. After another three months of rehabilitation, the doctors decided he could go home and recuperate.

Eric's insurance company flew him by air ambulance to Jersey, where once again he endured physiotherapy and walking exercises. Another three months passed before Eric could walk, first on crutches, then with a stick. Once discharged, he lived with his parents and brother, Curtis.

The dining room became Eric's downstairs bedroom, and during this period of recuperation, a social worker made several suggestions to his parents regarding other essential changes. Another two months passed before his doctor and his Occupational Therapist were both satisfied he could manage on his own. Slowly but surely, he regained his mobility and could soon walk without the stick. He and Curtis took short walks together and on one occasion were joined by Marion, a girlfriend of Curtis.

'Nothing serious,' Curtis informed Eric. Then, giving him a wink, added, 'Yet!'

Out of the blue, Eric received a letter from Gary, apologising that he hadn't been in touch sooner. Eric's parents had opened one of Gary's earlier notes and had written to inform him of the accident. In this latest letter, Gary told Eric that his dream had come true – well, almost. He had met and married Julia, a girl from Stevenage, whose father – wait for it – owned, not a haulage company, but a removal firm. And he was working there as a junior partner.

Gary then asked about Eric's driving skills and assured him of a job in the firm, should Eric ever return to the UK permanently. The letter contained an address and phone number, and that evening Eric phoned and spoke at length with Gary. He explained that lorry driving was out, but he hoped he'd soon be able to start driving his replacement car, bought and delivered by the insurance company. He would need to take a driving test before being allowed back on the road, and he hoped this would happen soon.

The correspondence and communication between the two dwindled to Christmas cards. Gary, by this time a father of two boys and a full partner in the firm, hoped that one day the two could somehow meet again. Eric, back driving again, found a job in his old firm as a local delivery man. No more Heavy Goods Vehicles, just a small white van.

Now at 31 years of age and still single, Eric had 'itchy feet'. He wanted to travel again, and then came his opportunity. A phone call from Gary informed him that his father-in-law had died, and that he and his wife Julia had ownership of the removals firm. It was now a very successful company which also specialised in storage.

'But I need someone of your experience to head up the transport department,' Gary continued. 'Would you consider a well-paid job in an up-and-coming removal and storage company, with all your travelling expenses paid?'

'This "well-paid" job,' asked Eric, 'are the wages negotiable? Say yes, and I will be on next Monday's plane.'

'Yes,' laughed Gary. 'Do you need any help with travelling money?'

'No,' replied Eric and, laughing, continued, 'I'll present you with an expense sheet.'

As the years passed, the firm grew, and Gary's two boys, Gary Junior and Philip (after his grandfather) were learning the business. Eric began dating and soon married Cynthia, one of the office staff. But when Eric and Cynthia's children, Richard and William, were still in primary school, Gary died of a heart attack, leaving behind a grieving family.

A few months later, Julia and a gentleman arrived in Eric's office.

'This is Brian Whittaker, our family solicitor,' Julia explained. 'We have been discussing the future of the business.

My boys are too young to, and I don't want to run the business. We have decided to place the business in your name with Gary Jr. and Philip as junior partners until you decide they are ready to take on a full partnership with you.'

Seeing the surprised expression on Eric's face, she continued, 'Please say you will. It will take a load off my mind and leave me free to get on with my "bucket list". Mr Whittaker will draw up the necessary documents, and all you need to do is place your signature beneath mine.' Julia smiled and looked at Eric pleadingly, who returned her smile.

'It will be my pleasure to help you complete your bucket list,' he replied, 'and undertake the training of my junior partners.'

With that, Brian Whittaker opened his briefcase and produced some papers.

'Oh, I knew you would say yes,' said Julia with tears in her eyes. 'Thank you.' She leaned across the desk and kissed Eric on both cheeks. 'I'll leave you in the capable of hands of Mr Whittaker.' She left the office.

* * * * * *

Although her brothers had stayed and worked in Birmingham and Lancaster following their university terms in those cities, Erin had joined a firm of solicitors in Stevenage and continued living with her parents. Following Eric's promotion, her dad was now a company director and in charge of recruiting and training, and he persuaded Erin to leave her employment and take a position with the removal company.

After considering the generous pay offer made by her uncle and dad, she joined the company as office manager. Her rise in wages meant she could now purchase an apartment in Stevenage, where her friend Lisa visited and often stayed over.

One day James came into her office with a grave expression on his face.

'What do you remember from your trips to Jersey?' he asked Erin. 'I know we haven't been there in over 10 years.'

'Well, I remember visiting Gran and Grandad,' Erin replied. Then, after a slight pause to grasp a memory, she continued, 'They were both in a nursing home, weren't they?'

'Yes,' replied James. 'Your gran had dementia, and Grandad couldn't cope. So, not long after, they both entered the nursing home, where your gran died.'

'That's right,' Erin recalled. 'You went to the funeral. Mum explained what had happened.'

'Your grandad had an amazing constitution, but for the last two years he was a victim of Alzheimer's disease. He died yesterday.'

'How sad,' responded Erin.' Are you going to the funeral?'

'Yes, so is Eric, along with Cynthia and your mum. So, you and the boys will be in charge. We'll be away for about a week.'

Then, with a thoughtful expression on her face, Erin said, 'I seem to remember seeing Gran and Grandad in our house,'

'No, not here,' her dad replied. 'I brought them for a holiday to Northern Ireland. They stayed in a guesthouse in Holywood. That was in 2005. You would have been about six then. It was just shortly after my demob. We all flew to Stevenage to take up my job with your Uncle Eric. Unfortunately, after your grandparents left to fly home and we promised to visit, the pressure of work made visiting Jersey difficult. Your Uncle Eric and family managed to make one visit just before Gran went into the nursing home. I didn't get to see them, much to...' He left the sentenced unfinished.

'Go on,' responded Erin.

After another pause during which James's face creased in a frown, he continued, 'With your grandparents in the nursing home,' he paused as if about to add something else but just coughed and went on, 'well, it took all of the price of their house and more to pay for their keep, but—'

At that, the telephone rang in James's office and, with a wave, he left Erin.

'Well, a holiday in Jersey,' Erin thought to herself. 'I will put it in my diary for next year, and perhaps look up the old homestead.'

This summer, she and Lisa planned to go and see the Eden Project and spend some time touring the West Country.

CHAPTER 2

Lisa googled Jersey and discovered some interesting facts. She knew that it was one of the Channel Islands, but what she learned about the war years amazed her. So, Lisa then looked on Amazon for a DVD on Jersey and eventually ordered one that looked interesting.

Excited about the forthcoming holiday, she phoned her friend.

'Hi Erin,' she told her. 'I looked up the history of Jersey, and although I knew about the German occupation, I learned so much more. Now I can't wait for our holiday. When would be a good time to go?'

'I have looked up several dates,' replied Erin, 'but now, with your new-found knowledge, I think we should go in May. The Liberation of Jersey is celebrated every year on the ninth of May. So what do you think?'

'Hey, that sounds good,' Lisa responded. 'I have sent for a DVD on Jersey, and we can view it together when it arrives on Tuesday.'

'Tuesday it is then,' said Erin. 'Popcorn and video, say about eight?'

'Eight's fine,' replied Lisa. 'I'll get in the wine.' And then, with a giggle, she added, 'Oh, I'm so excited!'

At 8.15am on May 3rd, 2018 an EasyJet flight with Lisa and Erin on board took off from London Luton Airport bound for Jersey. After watching the video, the girls had chosen to stay at the *Pomme d'Or* Hotel. They had learned that this hotel had been the German Naval Headquarters during the invasion of 1940, and that the German occupation had lasted until the liberation of the Channel Islands on May 9th, 1945.

The flight over, Lisa and Erin stepped down from the plane onto a sunny airport tarmac. In the Arrivals hall, they collected their cases and hired a taxi to Liberation Square, and the *Pomme d'Or* Hotel.

The girls chatted excitedly with the hotel receptionist as they checked in, and soon they were in their room overlooking the square. At the reception, Lisa had picked up some literature regarding the German occupation, which she placed on her bedside locker drawer to read later.

Over dinner, the girls excitedly discussed their holiday.

'By the way,' remarked Lisa, 'I remember you telling me that your family used to live here. Do you know where? And can I see where your dad was born?'

'Well,' replied Erin, 'let's look at our Jersey map later and see if I can recognise any place my dad may have mentioned.'

In their room later, Erin stretched out the map of Jersey and peered at various place names.

'There!' she exclaimed, pointing to a town in the north of the island. 'That is where my family lived. I remember Dad saying that he loved the beach near "Good Night" – and look, – *Bon Nuit.*'

'And *Bon Nuit* to you, too,' said Lisa, yawning. 'I'm tired. Let's make plans to visit *Bon Nuit* after breakfast. It's been a long day.'

'Ok,' responded Erin, 'but I bet that I am too excited to sleep.'

But sleep they both did.

After breakfast the next morning, the girls again studied the map, then Erin rang reception.

'Hello, this is room 214. Can you recommend a reasonably priced car hire company?' she asked.

'Of course,' the receptionist replied. 'We always recommend Jersey Motors. They are located nearby on Queen's Road, and quite reasonable.'

'Thank you,' responded Erin. She replaced the receiver and turned to Lisa. 'Now, let's go adventuring!'

* * * * * *

Hiring the car proved stress-free, and soon Erin was driving them out of St Helier towards *Bon Nuit*.

'Best place for information regarding your family would be the local pub,' Lisa ventured.

'Good idea,' replied Erin, 'and I could also murder a coffee. So, first stop a café, I think. Ok?'

'Sounds good,' said Lisa, 'and a wee bun.' She continued with a laugh, expanding the wee.

They pulled in at what proved to be a popular coach stop and found a table outside the *Bon Nuit* Restaurant and gift shop. Lisa ordered then brought coffee and cake to their table. They were chatting once again about Erin's family when the waiter came to collect their cups and plates. He turned away, then paused.

'Sorry,' he said, 'I couldn't help overhearing you mention the name Eric Pearce and *Bon Nuit* village.'

'Yes,' Erin interrupted, 'my name is Pearce.'

'Well, my mother's maiden was Pearce, and I had an uncle, Eric.'

'Did he have a serious car accident?' Erin asked.

'Yes!' the young man exclaimed. 'Then, when he recovered, he went to live in England.'

'This is amazing!' Erin responded. 'Can I meet your mother? And what's your name, cousin?'

'I am Charlie,' he answered, then added, 'Look, have another coffee on me, and I'll have a word with the boss about hopefully getting an hour off between now and lunchtime. That's our busiest period when we get loads of coaches arriving.'

All the time the conversation was taking place, an older man at a nearby table looked intently towards the girls. When

Charlie left, he rose and, after a brief hesitation, walked towards the car park. He stopped once to glance back at Lisa and Erin, then walked up the nearby slope and looked again in time to see the waiter approach the girls' table.

Charlie smiled at Erin. 'Right,' he said, 'enjoy your coffee, and I will collect you in about 15 minutes when I get cleared up, then I will take you to meet my mother and grandfather. Unfortunately, my dad died two years ago.'

'Oh, this is exciting!' exclaimed Erin as they supped their coffee.

'And what an amazing coincidence,' Lisa added.

* * * * * *

'Mum, let me introduce Erin,' began Joseph, 'Uncle Eric's niece and her friend, Lisa. They are here on holiday. Erin is keen to see where her dad's family lived.'

A shadow crossed the lady's face but quickly disappeared, replaced by a smile.

'Welcome, niece, I haven't seen you since you were a little girl,' she said.

'Well, thank you, and hello… Auntie,' Erin responded.

'Forget about auntie, please,' laughed Charlie's mother, 'it's Marion. Come in.'

'And this is my friend, Lisa.'

'Pleased to meet you, too,' Marion replied, and ushered the girls and Charlie into the front room where they all sat down.

His mother then gave Charlie a questionable look.

'Oh, the boss gave me time off to bring the girls here,' he explained, 'as long as I'm back in time for the dinner-time coaches.'

'Charlie, why don't you and Lisa say hello to your grandfather?' Marion suggested. 'Then put the kettle on and we will have some tea. There's a small cake in the cupboard and biscuits in the tin. I want a family chat with Erin.'

Turning to Lisa, she said, 'I hope you don't mind.'

'Not at all,' said Lisa. 'Come on, Charlie, it's teatime.'

With Charlie and Lisa away, Marion opened a drawer of a writing bureau and drew something out. She sat down opposite Erin, frowned, then spoke.

'I want to explain something before you start asking questions, Erin. Charlie is the son of your uncle, Curtis.' With that, she showed Erin a photograph. It was of her dad, Uncle Eric, and someone who looked remarkably like her father.

'The one on the left is your Uncle Curtis. He and your father were twins. Curtis and I were engaged to be married when he mysteriously disappeared. Unfortunately, I was two months' pregnant at the time. Your father or Eric hadn't mentioned this?'

'No, I didn't even know about you,' replied Erin, 'and nothing about the disappearance of Uncle Curtis.'

'I've heard nothing about or from Curtis since he disappeared. So, obviously he knows nothing about Charlie. My father, who we live with is very bitter, even after all the years that have passed. So, when I introduce you, don't be offended if he seems cold towards you.'

'I won't,' Erin assured her, 'I am so thrilled to know I have relatives still living in Jersey.'

Just then, Lisa knocked the door then poked her head in and said, 'Tea's ready.'

'Come here, Lisa,' said Erin. 'Look.' And she showed her the photograph. 'That's my dad and Uncle Eric. And that is my Uncle Curtis. An uncle I never knew I had, and he is Charlie's father.'

Marion interrupted, 'Curtis and I were not married. He mysteriously disappeared, leaving me pregnant. So, things are a still touchy, especially with Charlie's grandad. But let's go and eat. Erin, you can keep that photo. I have loads of the family and me.'

* * * * * *

The sound of the doorbell interrupted their conversation. They heard Charlie open the door and say, 'Hello, Uncle Phil.'

Then another voice, which Erin assumed belonged to his Uncle Phil, said gruffly, 'I'm here to see Dan.'

'Right,' Charlie responded. 'He is in the living room.'

Charlie then popped his head around the front-room door. 'Uncle Phil is here, and the tea is ready.'

'Thanks, son,' said Marion. 'We will join you in the kitchen after I take Erin in to meet your granddad.'

Marion rose, and Erin followed her into the living room.

'That's her, Dan!' exclaimed Phil. 'That's the girl I saw talking to Charlie. And I heard her say the name Pearce. She also called Charlie her cousin.'

Ignoring Phil, Marion said, 'Father, this is James Pearce's daughter Erin. She didn't know we existed until she met and spoke to Charlie at the *Bon Nuit* Café.'

'So, she doesn't know about Curtis?' Marion's father asked.

'She does now,' replied Marion. 'I have told her everything.'

'Everything?' asked her father.

'Yes, Dad, everything!' Marion responded. 'And if you come through to the kitchen, Charlie and Lisa have made tea.'

'Lisa is my friend,' replied Erin, 'and I am so pleased to meet you all.'

With that, she proffered her hand to Dan. After a pause, he took it. Then, to his astonishment, Erin leaned forward and kissed him on the cheek.

Suddenly, Dan burst out laughing.

'After what Phil told me, I did not expect to be civil to you. But, blow me down, you have taken the wind from my sails. Welcome, Miss Erin Pearce, to the Carstairs household. Let's have tea. Come on, Phil.'

Suddenly everyone spontaneously burst out laughing as they made their way to the kitchen.

CHAPTER 3

Later, after Charlie and Phil left, Dan, Marian, Erin, and Lisa sat in the living-room and shared stories. Lisa had very little to contribute, but Erin told of Eric's recovery and his partnership in the removal firm.

'I accompanied Curtis on a few occasions when he helped in Eric's rehabilitation,' Marion explained. 'But what about your family, Erin? I attended your dad's wedding to my work colleague, Grace.'

'Oh,' remarked Erin, 'so you were a schoolteacher like Mum?'

'And I still am, part-time,' Marion replied.

Erin then recounted her family history – the army travels, how her brothers were born in Ireland, how Uncle Eric had married into his friend Gary's removal family, then how he had become manager and part-owner of the company when Gary died.

'My dad works for Uncle Eric and he persuaded me to leave my job in a solicitor's office to manage the office staff and orders, etc.' She stopped. 'I have talked too much. Could we possibly visit my dad's old homestead?'

'Good idea,' said Marion. 'Poor Lisa is bored listening to all our tales.'

'I'll not come,' said Dan. 'It's a snooze time for me.'

* * * * * *

As the car drew into *Bon Nuit* village, Marion gasped. 'Wow! This area has changed over the past 20 years. It's been that length of time since I last visited. I used to come for supper each Sunday evening with Curtis. I even visited a few times after he disappeared, but not when my pregnancy started to show. All the small cottages have gone; even your grandparents' house has changed. The new owners have extended it outwards and upwards.'

'Nevertheless, could we explore?' Erin asked.

'Of course,' replied Marion. 'There's an old saying, "The cat can look at the queen".'

The three women left the car and walked into the village. As they passed the former Pearce dwelling, the front door opened and a lady appeared.

'Marion?' she called.

Marion turned. 'Well, bless my soul, if it isn't Catherine Williams.'

'Catherine Blake now,' the lady responded. 'I haven't seen you in years. Come on in for coffee.'

Marion looked at Erin, and both she and Lisa nodded.

'Catherine and I went to college together and attended the local dances held hereabouts,' explained Marian as they drank their coffees.

'Oh, we were the belles of the ball until Curtis swept her off her feet,' added Catherine. 'Did you and Curtis ever marry?'

'No,' replied Marion, 'but that's a story for another time. I suppose you know that this is his former home?'

'No!' exclaimed Catherine. 'My husband Alec bought this house as an investment, but after carrying out all the renovations, which took some time, we fell in love with it and the area. After our wedding, we moved here. That's about 20 years ago.'

'Well, let me introduce you to the granddaughter of the former owners, Miss Erin Pearce,' said Marion, 'and her friend Lisa. They are here on holiday and, for Erin, a nostalgic adventure.'

It became apparent during the conversations that Catherine knew nothing of Marion's circumstances, and with nothing disclosed, they said their farewells and continued the exploration of the village.

'So much has changed,' said Marion, 'and Catherine says most of the old cottages have gone and these,' she pointed to the new builds, 'are owned mostly by business families.'

'It's sad to see the old disappearing,' said Lisa, 'and in Kent, where we live, it's mostly the same. But the English still love their heritage, and many of the Kentish villages still retain their age-old character. You must visit some time and let us show you around.'

'Thanks, Lisa,' responded Marion, 'I will.'

As they walked back to the car, Erin was more than a little disappointed. She would love to have seen her grandparents' house as it had been in her family's time.

'I suppose,' she said, speaking her thoughts out loud, 'it doesn't always help going back to the past.'

'Well said,' remarked Marion. 'I felt quite heartsick at seeing the past gone.'

They drove back to Marion's house in silence. Erin and Lisa both declined to stay for an evening meal, saying that they could all perhaps meet up before the end of the holiday.

'Let me have your phone number,' said Erin,' and we will give you a call.'

Having recorded Marion's number in her iPhone, she and Lisa waved goodbye and headed back towards St Helier in their hire car.

Over dinner, Lisa remarked on how quiet Erin had become since returning from *Bon Nuit.*

'Yes, I'm sorry,' said Erin. 'Let's book a coach tour for tomorrow, and see the rest of the island.'

'Good idea,' Lisa responded, 'and we'll take a long walk this evening to see some of St Helier. I read about a lovely park,' she extracted a leaflet from her handbag, 'called the Howard Davis Park. The pictures look beautiful, and we could go there this evening.'

'That is also a good idea.' said Erin with a smile. 'You know,' she said, looking at Lisa's leaflet, 'suddenly I feel much brighter, and my excitement has returned.'

'Great!' exclaimed Lisa. 'Let's go!'

Her excited exclamations drew stares from the other diners, so Lisa gave the occupants a cheery wave, then linked her arm with Erin's and they headed out of the dining-room.

* * * * * *

The Howard Davis Park proved to be as beautiful as the leaflet suggested, and the girls strolled arm-in-arm in the evening sunlight, as Lisa read the park's history.

'Apparently, Howard Davis created it in memory of his son who died in the First World War, and there are war graves somewhere. Ah, there they are!'

The war graves had simple wooden crosses rather than stone, and the girls later found out that was because the islanders had petitioned for them to remain that way.

CHAPTER 4

Next morning after breakfast, the girls walked across Liberation Square to a kiosk advertising coach tours. The waitress at breakfast had suggested the kiosk tours cost less than booking at the hotel.

'But don't say I told you,' she said with a smile.

They decided on an all-island tour which left from outside their hotel at 10am, returning at 5pm. The coach arrived at 9.45, and they joined the queue of waiting passengers. During the journey, the driver gave excellent talks on a variety of places and the driver stopped at several to allow the passengers to take photos. Erin and Lisa received vouchers to allow a discount at Jersey Gold, where they made a few purchases.

To their surprise, the coach pulled in at *Bon Nuit* for a lunch stop where, once again, they met and spoke briefly to Charlie. After lunch, the tour continued around the island with more information and comfort stops.

Back at their hotel, Erin tipped the driver as they alighted from the coach. They both agreed on how worthwhile and enjoyable the trip had proved to be, providing them with much more information about the island, some of its famous inhabitants, and the places visited.

After dinner, Erin and Lisa walked along the seafront and back via the town. They were so engrossed in sightseeing that they didn't notice the photographer.

Back at the hotel, they enjoyed a cup of hot chocolate then settled into their beds. Lisa continued to read through the leaflets she had gathered, but soon Erin's breathing told her she was fast asleep.

* * * * * *

Wednesday – midway through the holiday – dawned slightly cloudy. The rain came during breakfast, and Erin suggested that she would phone Marion.

'I'll invite her and Charlie for dinner this evening,' she said.

'That would be nice,' said Lisa, 'but I'm sure the rain will stop soon, and I would like to visit a bookshop. I want to read more about Jersey, and I noticed a book mentioned in one of the leaflets I read last night.'

'Won't you find all you want to know on Google?' asked Erin.

'I prefer the feel of a book and physically turning pages,' Lisa replied, 'and I always did love reading proper books.' She emphasised the word 'proper'.

'Ah, me,' responded Erin, 'I'm a Kindle fan.'

'All to their own,' was Lisa's reply. 'Look, the rain has stopped, and I can see a glimmer of the sun. Go on and phone Marion, and I will fetch our macs, just in case.'

In the bookshop, Lisa browsed and soon found the book she wanted. While she paid, Erin told her that she needed the toilet.

Lisa opened the book and walked out of the shop into the pale sunlight to wait for her friend. Suddenly, she felt something being prodded into her back and a voice said, 'Don't look round. Walk towards the car.'

A car had pulled up at the kerb, the driver alighted and opened the rear door.

'Not a sound, just get in,' said the voice.

Once in the rear seat of the car, her companion tied a scarf around Lisa's eyes, then the driver started the engine and drove off.

Erin exited the shop just in time to see the car move away from the kerb with a blindfolded Lisa in the rear. She quickly memorised the registration number and entered it into her iPhone then dialled 999 and asked for the police.

When they arrived, Erin gave the police an accurate description of the vehicle – model and registration number – but unfortunately, she couldn't describe the kidnappers, except that the man in the back seat with Lisa had a prominent nose and chin.

'He reminded me of Punch, from my days at the seaside,' Erin remarked, then burst into tears.

Later, she phoned Marion and cancelled dinner with an excuse about a double booking, but promised to be in touch.

* * * * * *

Following a long and sometimes bumpy journey, the car stopped. Lisa felt hands grab her, quite gently, and draw her from the vehicle. As her kidnapper guided her along a smooth path, he whispered in her ear, 'Get ready for a surprise.' Then he laughed softly.

'Step up,' he commanded. And even though she was still blindfolded, Lisa knew she had come from sunlight into a dark place. She heard someone in front of her say, 'Lights, Jim.'

Then her abductor removed her blindfold, and two voices shouted, 'Surprise!'

As her eyes grew accustomed to the light, Lisa heard the person in front of her say, 'Oh-oh! Fellows, not so much a surprise as a mistake. Put the coffee on. This girl is not Erin.'

Lisa stared at the figure and said, 'I know you. I recognise you from a photograph. You're Erin's Uncle Curtis!'

* * * * * *

'What photograph?' asked Curtis. 'And who are you?'

Lisa reached for her phone. 'Why not talk to the one you meant to kidnap?'

With that, she pressed Erin's quick-dial number, and her friend answered immediately.

'Lisa, where are you? I saw you in a car with a scarf over your eyes and—'

'Erin, Erin,' interrupted Lisa, 'hush, hush. Just listen. I am perfectly safe; It was all a joke. Now, without any more questions, here is what I want you to do. In about half an hour, stand at the steps of our hotel and the same car which you saw take me will call and pick you up.'

'But… but—'

'No,' interrupted Lisa again, 'no buts. You are in for a nice surprise. And Erin, wear your red scarf on your head. We don't any more mistakes.'

With that, and waiting for no more objections, Lisa ended the call.

CHAPTER 5

For a few moments, Erin stared at her phone wanting to call back, but then remembered the police. She rang the police station and, after identifying herself, apologised for the inconvenience and asked that they take no further action. After telling Erin she could be in trouble for wasting police time, the annoyed desk sergeant rang off.

Still worried, she made herself a cup of coffee and waited for the rendezvous time to come round.

* * * * *

In response to Lisa's questioning, Curtis explained that they were in a cottage on the borough of St Lawrence, in a place called The Grove.

'I recognised Erin from a contact I had in England,' Curtis explained. 'He passed me information about my brothers, and sent me pictures. He was a former private detective, now retired. We met in a hospital in France.' Curtis frowned, then laughed, 'But that's a long story which I will keep it until Erin arrives.'

Kyle left to collect Erin, while Curtis poured Lisa another coffee and indicated the other occupant of the room. 'Oh, and this is Carl – like Kyle, a helper from England.'

After a while, they heard the car draw up to the door of the cottage and Curtis turned and faced the fire. The door opened, and a red-scarfed Erin entered and ran to Lisa. After a hug, she said, 'Now, what is this? My driver refused to tell me anything.'

'Sit down, pet,' replied Lisa. 'I want to introduce you to someone.'

With that Curtis turned to face the now seated girls.

'Erin,' continued Lisa, 'meet your Uncle Curtis.'

Erin's mouth dropped open in amazement as she recognised the man from the photo which she hastily withdrew from her handbag.

'I don't understand,' she said, looking at the photo and then back at Curtis. 'It is you, but why did you kidnap Lisa?'

'Hello, my dear niece,' replied Curtis. 'That was a mistake. It was you my silly friends should have abducted. I wanted to surprise and meet you.'

Erin rose and approached her uncle. 'You are the spitting image of my dad, but I just don't understand.'

'Never mind,' Curtis responded. 'Let me embrace my never-forgotten niece.'

And with a little sob, Erin stepped into her uncle's arms.

'Come,' said Curtis. 'Although it is summer, I keep a fire burning. The cottage, to me, feels a little cold and damp.'

Kyle and Carl left the room as Curtis motioned the girls to a small settee. He sat opposite them in an armchair.

'On a trip to France many years ago, I foolishly became involved with a drug-smuggling gang. Dangerous work, but the money was good. My family knew nothing of this; they thought I had a job as a courier between a firm in Jersey and one in France. As a family, and including my fiancée Marion, we sat up late to welcome in the year 2000 and to see if any of the prophesied disasters would occur. You two would have just about been born.'

'Yes,' said Erin, 'we were both born in 1999.'

'Well,' continued Curtis, 'at 2am, and with no disasters announced, we all retired. At six o'clock I awoke when my mobile received a text advising me to leave Jersey and get to France ASAP. The text contained a designated code sign which I knew meant danger. I left a cryptic note for Marion saying I had to leave on an urgent trip to France and would be in touch; Marion had stayed overnight in our spare room.'

In his continuing story, Curtis told the girls how he caught the early ferry to St Malo and travelled to the arranged rendezvous, where he met with his confederates. The police had raided the house used as drug storage and had confiscated drugs and money. Two of the gang were arrested, but not before they had barricaded themselves in and sent off a text message to the primary drug co-ordinator.

Erin interrupted the story to ask, 'Did the police not interview your family in Jersey?'

Curtis smiled. 'The person the police were looking for didn't exist. In France, working with the drug cartel, I used a false name and a false Jersey address.'

Curtis continued his story. 'I knew that one of my closest friends in the group, Jonas, a Haitian, was in a Paris hospital recovering from an operation. So, when the group decided to split, I offered to stay in Paris using my proper name and wait for Jonas to recover and somehow get him out of France. I decided that even using my name, contacting Marion or family might place them in danger. So, reluctantly, I decided to disappear. It was cowardly, but at that time it seemed best. I suppose I'd hoped to get in touch at a later date.'

'Wait,' interrupted Erin, 'I have a feeling this story will get more interesting. Do you mind if I record it?'

'No,' laughed Curtis. 'Maybe you can turn it into a novel someday. My fictitious name, of course.'

'Which was?' asked Erin.

'Jake Canning,' replied Curtis. 'Not sure where that came from.'

Erin took a photo of Curtis, then plugged in her phone and set it to record.

'Right, "The Life Story of Jake Canning",' she announced.

CHAPTER 6

Curtis had visited Jonas in the hospital, only to learn that his condition had deteriorated. Jonas reached and brought a bag from beneath his bed, and pleaded with Curtis to get the contents to his family in Haiti. 'Believe me, Curtis, I'm not going to make it. All you need to know is inside.'

With that, Jonas fell asleep, and Curtis sat with him for a while. He then heard an English voice from the next curtained bed, arguing with a doctor.

When the doctor left, Curtis left his sleeping friend, peeped behind the curtain, and said, 'Hello.' The patient looked a sorry sight. His bruised face and bandaged arm suggested he'd had an accident, but he motioned for Curtis to sit down, saying that it was lovely to hear an English voice.

The man explained that his name was Richard Cummings and that he was a private detective on an assignment in Paris. The previous night, Richard had had an encounter with three thugs, who beat him up and stole his wallet, phone, and watch. He'd regained consciousness in the hospital, where he was receiving treatment. Richard explained that the row with the doctor had occurred because the hospital learned he couldn't pay for his treatment.

Curtis suddenly stopped listening as an idea flashed into his mind. He realised that Richard had stopped talking, so he ventured a proposal. He would pay for Richard's treatment if he would go back to England and search for Curtis's family. Richard readily agreed, and the exchanged details.

At that point, the police arrived looking for Jonas. As the doctor led them to his bed, he explained that Jonas was a very ill man.

Curtis motioned to Richard to be quiet, and listened as the police said they would leave an officer by Jonas' bedside. Curtis chatted to a surprised Richard in French, then said 'Au revoir', picked up Jonas's bag, and left the ward.

The next day, he rang the hospital to learn that Jonas had died in the night and that the police wanted to talk to his visitor if he would get in touch. Curtis knew then that the time had come for him to disappear once again.

Using his Jersey passport, Curtis booked a flight to Haiti, having checked that nothing in Jonas's bag would land him in trouble. The bag contained money, photos, and the details of his family.

In Haiti, Curtis looked up Jonas's family and found his sister. He passed on the news of the young man's death, and handed over the bag. He then gave her the name and telephone number of the Paris hospital, wished her well, and bade her *adieu*.

* * * * * *

But in Haiti, things went pear-shaped. Curtis got drunk, and his drinking companion named Jaquez started a fight in the pub. During the battle, Curtis received a knockout punch and came to in a police van, minus his jacket, wallet, and passport. Someone in the pub must have taken them. So, when asked his name, Curtis reverted to his pseudonym – Jack Canning.

Erin paused her recording when Jim appeared and announced, 'Dinner!'

Kyle and Carl had prepared a lovely fish meal, which the group enjoyed, then they all helped clear up before sitting down for coffee in front of the fire.

Once again, Erin switched on the recorder, and Curtis continued with his story.

During the fight in the pub, a man had died. And although Jaquez had struck the fatal blow, he and Curtis were both convicted of manslaughter and sentenced to ten years in Port-au-Prince jail. Which is where he met two men, Jim and Erik, who were serving time for smuggling.

Curtis explained that Jaquez had died in prison from pneumonia, after serving three years of his sentence. Then, in 2010 came freedom.

'That year the island suffered a severe earthquake, during which the part of the prison containing us collapsed. Miraculously, about a dozen prisoners survived, including Erik, Jim, and me,' he said.

The three escapees hid by the docks and eventually discovered a cargo boat bound for Portugal where Jim had lived and worked for two years. He spoke a little of the language. With some of the crew killed in a dockside bar during the earthquake, Jim had no problem persuading the ship's Portuguese captain to take them on as crew.

Their outfits showed the captain that they were escaped convicts, but he found them spare garments from the locker room and, with his cargo loaded, he cast off. The reduced crew were made to work hard, but the three travellers didn't mind. Most of the journey took place in darkness, arriving at dawn into Lisbon harbour.

As the unloading commenced, the captain appeared on deck and motioned for Curtis, Jim and Erik to follow him. Another deckhand appeared and accompanied them to a container at the rear of the ship. The captain opened the doors and, speaking slowly in Portuguese, explained to Jim what would happen next. Jim turned to his companions and explained that they were to get inside the container and eventually the crane would lift and park it on a spot which the deckhand, Carlos, would indicate. He would then open the door to their freedom.

The captain then produced a wad of banknotes which he handed to Jim. In broken English, he said that it was not much, but would get them somewhere.

Carlos indicated for them to enter the container, then he closed the doors. A little apprehensive, the trio waited then grabbed the door latches to hang on as they felt the container swinging into the air.

CHAPTER 7

Once released from the container by Carlos, Jim thanked him, and the deckhand replied, 'Vaya con Dios', which Jim recognised as Spanish for 'God go with you'.

The three comrades made their way to the dockyard entrance and passed through unchallenged. Once outside, Jim led the way into the city and to a Vodafone shop, where he used some of the cash to purchase a pay-as-you-go mobile and SIM card. With the phone ready, Jim closed his eyes as if in thought and then dialled a number.

He spoke in Portuguese, introduced himself, and asked to talk to Carol. Even at a distance, Curtis could hear a woman's voice shouting and asking questions. Jim finally managed to explain his whereabouts and explained that he and two friends needed help.

When he ended the call, Jim told the others that they were to stay there and his friend Carol would collect them. He explained that Carol and her family had lived in Portugal for many years, and Jim had at one time worked for her father in his store.

After a short wait, a car drew up beside them and a lady, who Curtis assumed was Carol, got out. She walked towards Jim and frowned. 'Jim?' she asked.

'Forgive my appearance, but yes, it's me,' he replied.

Carol stepped forward to hug him but hastily drew back. 'Oh dear,' she remarked, 'I think a clean-up first, and then you'll get your hug. Now, into the car.'

Carol drove out of the city but pulled into a supermarket car park.

'Now,' she said, producing a notepad and pen from the glove compartment. 'Write down your shirt, trousers, and shoe sizes against each of your names.'

The men obeyed and handed the notebook and pen back to Carol.

'Right, I am going into the shop,' she said, 'and I want you three to get out of the car, but stay put and leave the doors open.' Carol laughed as she walked away.

Half an hour later, Carol returned carrying four bags, which she put into the boot of her car.

'Right, lads, back in the car,' she commanded, and they willingly obeyed.

After a short drive, Carol turned into a driveway leading to a large house.

'I recognise this,' said Jim 'You never moved?'

She stopped the car outside the front door of the house, and replied, 'No, I lived here until my father died, then I married. You spoke to my husband, Jim. We decided to reopen the house and live here. OK, out you get.'

The front door opened, and a swarthy gentleman appeared and smiled a greeting.

Carol kissed him then explained, 'This is my husband, Lucas. Portuguese born and bred.'

Lucas shook hands with each of the men, then stepped aside and motioned them to follow Carol inside.

'Now, gentlemen,' she said, 'there are two shower rooms in this house, one downstairs and one upstairs. You can decide who goes first and to which one.'

Jim told Curtis and Erik to go first, and said he would chat – from a distance – to Carol and Lucas.

Before they headed off, Carol took the bags from the boot of the car and laid them on the floor in order in front of the three men.

'These contain shirts, trousers, pyjamas, and shoes. Once you've showered and dressed, I will take you to a barber to sort out your hair and beards.'

'How do we repay you?' asked Jim. 'All we have is this.' And he produced what remained of the captain's money.

'Ah, you're not to worry about that,' replied Carol. 'I have a cunning plan.'

Lucas showed Curtis to the downstairs shower room, and Jim led Erik to the one upstairs.

Once Curtis reappeared, Jim left for his shower.

When all three were finished, Carol led them through to a very comfortable lounge.

'Jim has brought us up to date with your circumstances,' she said, 'and how you came to be here.'

'So, what is your cunning plan?' asked Curtis.

'Well, I think it will most likely concern you, Curtis,' Carol replied. 'But we will discuss it after dinner, which we will now go and prepare.'

As the couple left the room, Curtis excused himself to go to the bathroom.

'What are your plans?' Jim asked, perched on a seat near the window.

'I am heading to Slovakia and home,' replied Erik.

'Well, you had better have this,' said Jim, and produced the money. 'I won't need it because I'm home.' And he swept the room with his arms before handing Erik the notes.

'But what about Curtis?' asked Erik.

'Oh, I think Curtis can look after himself,' Jim replied. 'Now put it away before he comes back, and say nothing. You and I are the mates here.'

Erik pocketed the money just before Curtis returned and Carol announced that their meal was ready.

* * * * *

Following the delicious dinner, they returned to the lounge to drink coffee.

'Now, before I tell you my plan,' said Carol, 'what are yours? Oh, I know Jim is staying here. He asked for permission while you two were showering, and I could use his help.'

'I am going home to Slovakia,' said Erik, 'after I have settled my account here.'

'That won't be necessary,' responded Carol. 'Curtis will do that.'

'I don't know how,' said Curtis, looking confused. 'Jim has the only cash available.'

'No,' countered Jim, 'I made an executive decision and gave the rest to Erik. It will help him find his way home.'

'I don't want any money,' said Carol. 'I just need Curtis to help Lucas. Let me explain.'

* * * * * *

Carol's husband was a government courier, and his next task involved taking documents to London and collecting a package there.

She informed them that Lucas could speak a few European languages, but little English, and she had considered accompanying him. Her workload, however, made that impossible, so Curtis was a godsend.

CHAPTER 8

'Now, you three – barber.' Carol loaded her passengers into a sweeter smelling car and drove once more to the supermarket.

'Ivan is a Russian barber and very good,' she explained. 'He has a shop at the rear of the supermarket. I will leave you with him while I do some more shopping.'

Inside the barber's shop, Carol spoke with Ivan, handed him money, then waved the boys goodbye. One by one, they sat on the barber's chair, and their unruly hair and beards disappeared.

They met Carol as they exited the barbershop.

'My, oh my,' she laughed. 'What a difference.'

* * * * * *

They stayed with Carol and Lucas for three days, during which she made several phone calls.

'Now, gentlemen,' she said, 'another trip. You are having your pictures taken.'

This time, Carol headed the car in a different direction, to the small town of Aveiro. They stopped outside a carpenter's workshop where, once inside, Carol handed the workman a note. After reading it, he told her to wait, then he exited through a door at the rear of the building. A short while later, the man returned and signalled for the group to come. He pointed to a door at the end of a corridor, which they discovered opened into a photographic studio.

They were greeted by a lady who introduced herself in English as Tanya. She photographed Curtis, Jim, and Erik, shook hands with Carol, and said to give her a week.

In the car, Carol explained that Tanya would prepare three passports with brand new names for them. Curtis, Jim, and Erik would no longer exist.

A week later they were once again in Tanya's studio looking at their passports and their new names. Curtis became Jeremy Craig; Jim was James Wallace; and Erik was Andrej Kovac. Tanya advised them to memorise and practise writing their new names before signing the passports. Then she wished them luck and said goodbye.

* * * * * *

For two days, the men practised writing and memorising their new names until Carol felt they were ready for their next step.

'As you may have noticed, Jim is keeping his first name to avoid errors. And, Andrej, have this.' She handed Andrej an envelope. 'Inside you'll find identification papers and some Slovakian money. So, as soon as you are packed, you can be on your way.'

'James is staying here with me as my handyman, and Jeremy will accompany Lucas to London this afternoon. He has his instructions.' Jeremy received another envelope. 'Now let's have some lunch. Just sandwiches and cake.'

* * * * * *

Carol ran Andrej to the train station and waved him off. Next, she took Jeremy and Lucas to the airport, where she watched until their plane took off. Along with the instructions, the envelope she'd given Jeremy contained a considerable amount of cash. Using the little bit of English he could muster, Lucas explained that the Portuguese government were paying.

The first stop Curtis, now Jeremy, made was to a Mobile Phone Centre, where he purchased a pay-as-you-go phone and SIM. Lucas then phoned Carol to say they had arrived safely and were on their way to the hotel. He gave Jeremy Carol's mobile number, explaining in his faltering English that she wanted him to phone her.

Once settled into their rooms at the hotel, Jeremy phoned Carol. During their conversation, she told him that he need not return with Lucas, as long as he saw him safely to the plane. Jeremy thanked her for all she had done and for the money, and said he had a contact to find somewhere in England.

The following morning, using the name Jeremy, he escorted Lucas to Government House, where they showed their passports and Jeremy explained Lucas's lack of English. The official produced an interpreter and took Lucas to another room. After about half an hour, Lucas emerged and the official thanked Jeremy for his help and escorted them to the door.

Jeremy hailed a taxi, and they headed for the airport where Jeremy purchased a ticket for Lucas on the Lisbon flight scheduled for 12.30pm, so they both sat down at a table for lunch.

* * * * * *

With Lucas safely onboard his plane, Jeremy now reverted to his Curtis passport and checked in at a Premier Inn. From his inside jacket, he produced some saved notes, one of which contained Richard Cummings' mobile number. Hoping the number hadn't changed, he dialled, but there was no answer. He waited a while and tried again – same result.

Later that evening, he tried again; this time, a lady answered. Curtis introduced himself and explained his association with Richard. The woman informed him that she was Richard's daughter and that he was seriously ill in Leeds General Infirmary. Curtis thanked her and rang off without any further explanation.

Next morning, he checked out and hired a car and began the long drive to Leeds. Curtis made the journey without a break, then sought out a Premier Inn where he booked a night's stay.

Tired and hungry, he had dinner then collapsed onto his bed and slept.

At 7am, after a coffee and a shower, Curtis went for breakfast. In the lounge, he Googled Eric Pearce. The website for the storage depot appeared, along with names of the directors and managers of the firm. Curtis copied the names into his phone's notebook.

The website contained no personal information, so he hoped Richard Cummings could help.

Next, Curtis called up the address and visiting times for the Leeds General Infirmary, then decided to do a little shopping. At the nearest shopping centre, he purchased a watch, two shirts, a pair of trousers, and a small case.

Back at the café beside the Premier Inn, he had lunch then went back to his room and packed the case with all but his pyjamas. He then headed to the Leeds General.

Visiting time had just begun as he parked and walked to the information desk where he asked for Richard Cummings' ward.

A lady was sitting by Richard's bed as Curtis approached. When he introduced himself, it turned out that she was the daughter he had spoken to the previous day.

Richard stared at him. 'Curtis, where on earth have you been?'

Curtis explained that for personal reasons he had had to leave the country and had lost his mobile phone.

Richard asked his daughter, Joan, to give Curtis the key and instructions he had left with her for safekeeping. She opened her shoulder bag and produced a bulky envelope.

'I thought you might turn up either yesterday or today, so I brought this with me,' she said, handing the envelope to Curtis. 'My father took a slight stroke in March, but had worked up until then, and mostly for you. My husband, John, did all the other assignments. He now runs the agency.'

'Everything you asked of me is in there,' Richard croaked.

Curtis thanked them both, wished Richard well and left, knowing he would not see Richard again.

CHAPTER 9

In his Premier Inn room, Curtis opened the envelope. Inside he found notes and photographs covering years of family history. In the photos, he recognised his brothers and Richard had marked their children's names. Suddenly, Curtis felt homesick. He longed to see Marion again and catch up with her.

The latest update, dated February 2018, informed him that his niece Erin and her friend had booked a holiday in Jersey, his home island.

The following morning, his mobile rang. The caller identified himself as John Graham, Richard Cummings' son-in-law who, as Richard's partner, had inherited most of their clients. He wondered if Curtis had remained in Leeds and, if so, could they meet up?

Curtis gave him the address of the Premier Inn and John arranged a time to meet in the hotel's lounge that afternoon.

Later that day, over coffee John revealed that he had a client in Jersey who needed help.

'Richard thought that, as you originally came from there, you could help him,' John said.

He explained that his friend, William Cairns, was originally from Ireland but living and working In St Helier.

'He knows his wife is cheating on him, but can't prove it,' John went on. 'William received a promotion within his firm, and subsequently has been working longer hours, putting a strain on their social life. Along with that, his wife makes excuses to go out in the evenings.'

John explained that all he needed Curtis to do was to take photos and, if possible, discreetly follow the wife. And he produced two photographs – one of William, and one of his wife, Zena.

'Send him the pictures and a report, and there will be no other involvement,' he said. 'If, of course, you can capture the cheating couple together, and if, indeed, her activities involve cheating.'

John assured Curtis that he would have no other involvement and that there would be financial recompense.

Curtis thought for a while as he studied the photos. The idea of going back to Jersey excited him, and he still had his fake Jeremy passport which he could use. The extra money would come in useful. And a niece he had never known would be in Jersey at this time, and it would be nice to meet her perhaps. Weighing up all the advantages, Curtis agreed.

John heaved a sigh of relief. His workload had mounted up recently, and Jersey did not sound like a promising adventure to him. He shook Curtis by the hand, gave him an envelope detailing his instructions and expected pay, and then took a camera from his bag and handed it over.

After John had left, Curtis went back to his room and opened the envelope. A phew escaped his lips as he counted out one thousand pounds. He laughed; he was now a private detective.

That evening, sitting in the hotel bar, Curtis heard two men discussing their redundancy and moaning about being out of work. Deciding that help in Jersey might be useful, he offered to buy the men a drink and said he had a proposition to put to them, one which included money. During their conversation, Curtis learned that both men had families and could use any extra cash, providing it came legally.

Curtis explained his plans for Jersey. The job would only take a few days, for which they would each receive five hundred pounds. He outlined his task and felt that more than one person would make the job easier. The two men introduced themselves as Carl Johnson and Kyle Bradford.

* * * * * *

Families informed, bags packed, passports at the ready, Kyle, Carl, and Curtis – now travelling as Jeremy – purchased a one-way flight to Jersey. Most hotel rooms were booked due to the island's Liberation celebrations, but Curtis had discovered a small hotel with vacancies in the borough of St Clements, so booked two rooms.

When they arrived in Jersey, Curtis hired a car at the airport and they drove to their hotel and checked in. Thanks to Richard's thorough investigation, Curtis knew that the girls were staying at the *Pomme d'Or* Hotel. So, the following morning, he and his companions parked the car in St Helier, and he tasked Carl and Kyle with finding William and Zena's apartment, while he positioned himself in the *Pomme d'Or* reception and waited.

Eventually, the lift door opened and two girls exited and walked to a small table where one picked up leaflets. As they turned towards the hotel entrance, Curtis discreetly captured a photo of Erin.

Back at the car, he found Carl and Kyle waiting. They reported seeing Zena leave her apartment building and catch a bus to somewhere called St Brelade.

'Right,' said Curtis, 'we begin our observations this evening. Which of you drives?'

'We both do.' said Kyle.

'Ok, but drive carefully,' replied Curtis, handing the keys to Kyle, 'as you're not insured. I will spend the day in St Helier, so come back and park here at about 6.30pm and meet me at the Liberation Square.'

He pointed out the square to his colleagues, then watched as they drove off.

With his mind full of memories, Curtis caught a bus to *Bon Nuit* and sat in the café there drinking coffee and admiring the sea views he had known so well. So many times he and Marion had walked the promenade or lain on the beach. Occasionally they had made love in the dunes. Suddenly, and to his surprise, tears filled his eyes.

Curtis swiftly wiped them away as a young man approached his table and gave him a refill of coffee. Curtis wondered why the young man's face seemed familiar, but shrugged and left the café to catch his return bus to St Helier.

* * * * * *

Curtis told Kyle to wait in the car, and he and Carl would take turns following Zena. Carl led the way to the woman's apartment, and they watched as she emerged from the building around 7.30pm. Curtis instructed Carl to follow a short distance behind her, while he walked on the opposite pavement at a discreet distance. After turning into two side-streets, Zena entered a building with a familiar sign above the door. Curtis signalled Carl to wait, and he crossed the street.

After telling Carl to continue following Zena if she came out, Curtis then entered the building. The banner above the desk exhibited the familiar sign, St Jude's Care Centre.

'Hello,' Curtis addressed the young lady at the desk, 'does your centre use volunteers?'

'We do indeed,' she replied. 'Are you interested?'

'No, but my wife is,' lied Curtis, 'and I thought I would find out some details.'

'Of course,' responded the lady, and handed him some leaflets. 'These will tell your wife all about us. Have her call in for a chat; we are always looking for volunteer support.'

Curtis thanked her and turned to leave just as Zena exited the building.

Carl prepared to follow her, but Curtis indicated that he should return to the car while he hurried after Zena himself. A few blocks later, Zena stopped at an apartment building, and Curtis strolled passed as she rang a bell.

When Zena entered the building, Curtis went back and noted the name located by the doorbell – Mrs Catherine Smyth. Just then, the door opened and a young woman appeared.

'Excuse me,' said Curtis, 'I saw my friend Zena go in, and I urgently need to speak to her. Do you know who it is she is visiting?'

'Oh yes,' the woman replied, 'she is with Mrs Smyth.'

'Do you think she would mind if I called?' he asked.

'No,' the girl laughed. 'Catherine loves visitors.'

'Thank you,' said Curtis, and made as if to ring the bell. When she had gone, he turned away smiling to himself, and made his way back to the car.

The three men continued to check Zena's activities for two more days, but found no male involvement. Curtis photographed her movements and the places she visited, and wrote a detailed report to Richard which he posted off.

'There's one more assignment before you head home,' Curtis told Carl and Kyle. He had looked for and found a cottage to rent, so now he outlined his plan to kidnap Erin.

CHAPTER 10

'So ends my story,' Curtis informed Erin, who switched off her phone recorder.

'Oh, by the way, I received an update from John Graham with a bit more cash and telling me to keep the camera. All is well with William and Zena, so all's well that ends well.'

'Wow!' remarked Lisa. 'I'm glad I heard all of this. Thank you for kidnapping me,' she continued with a laugh.

'No,' said Erin, 'your story isn't over yet. Send your friends home but stay here a few days more. It's time you and your family were reunited.'

'Oh, I don't think Marion would welcome me after all this time,' Curtis replied.

'You might be surprised,' said Erin. 'Will you trust me to find out?'

Curtis just raised his hands, made a face, and shrugged. 'Who's for coffee?'

'No thanks,' said Erin. 'Now, ask one of your mates to take us back to our hotel, please. Oh, and give me your mobile number.'

Erin embraced her uncle, and Lisa gave him a friendly hug before they departed with Carl – the one with the Punch-like appearance – driving.

* * * * * *

Back in their hotel, the girls discussed the best way forward.

'The school will be closed tomorrow for Liberation Day. Let's invite her for morning coffee,' suggested Lisa.

'Yes,' replied Erin thoughtfully. 'But not here. I will phone her, and we could hire a car again and invite Marion to meet us at the *Bon Nuit* Café. There we can sound her out, and maybe Joseph, too. Although it will probably come as a shock to him.'

'You're on,' said Lisa. 'The parades don't get underway here until the afternoon. So, let's do it.'

Erin picked up her mobile and called Marion. 'Hello, Marion, Erin here. What are your plans for Liberation Day?'

'Oh, hello Erin,' Marion replied. 'I had planned to bring my dad in late morning, why?'

'Could we meet you at the café before you leave? I have a proposition,' said Erin. 'We could drive up there for morning coffee, say about 10.30?'

'Intriguing. You can come here if you like,' Marion suggested.

'No,' said Erin, 'I think you would prefer meeting at the café.'

'Hmmm, "Curiouser and curiouser," said Alice,' Marion laughed. Ok then, that will do.'

Erin then phoned the car hire company and arranged to collect a car the following morning.

The next morning, all went according to plan and the girls collected the car and stopped briefly at an electronic store before going on to meet Marion at the *Bon Nuit* Café for coffee.

Erin began, 'I want to show you something and someone I met recently.'

Opening her phone to the photo of Curtis, she showed it to Marion.

The woman stared for a long time at the picture before speaking. 'I don't understand,' she said. 'How did you speak to him recently? And where?'

Erin did not answer, but said, 'I have on this phone a fascinating story which I have transferred to this tape recorder. We listened to it on the way here, and it comes over clearly. I'd like you to listen to it before deciding whether you want to pursue it,' said Erin.

'The gentleman in the photo planned to kidnap Erin for a joke,' interrupted Lisa, 'but his pal kidnapped me by mistake. Later, Erin joined us, and the story began.'

'Do you want to hear it?' Erin asked.

Marion looked wary. 'I think I must,' she replied.

'What time did you think of going to St Helier?' asked Erin.

'I told him 11.30, 'said Marion, 'so I think I will listen to this later today, after I take Dad to see the celebrations.' She sighed. 'I think that after 18 years I can put Curtis off for another while.' She smiled and got up from the table. 'And thank you.'

Erin and Lisa drove back to St Helier and parked the hire car as close as possible to the hotel, then Erin phoned Curtis and put him in the picture, telling him to wait for an update.

'I will be in St Helier this afternoon,' he told Erin, 'but I will give your hotel a wide berth.'

* * * * * *

The Liberation Celebrations proved as spectacular as the girls thought they would be, and they thoroughly enjoyed going around the various stalls. They saw no sign of either Curtis or Marion, and after dinner collapsed on their beds exhausted.

Erin heard nothing from Marion that evening, but after breakfast, the woman appeared in the hotel foyer. The girls were just leaving the dining room when they saw Marion talking to the receptionist, who pointed in their direction.

Marion approached them and handed Erin back her recorder.

'An amazing story, which brought me to tears,' Marion admitted. 'I want to meet him before telling him about Joseph. I assume he doesn't know?'

'We said nothing to him before the recording about either you or Joseph,' Erin assured her. 'Let me contact him and arrange a meeting. Would you like to visit him at his cottage?'

'Oh,' exclaimed Marion, 'he has a cottage?'

'Rented,' explained Erin. 'Let me phone him. Why don't you and Lisa go for a coffee?'

Curtis answered her call immediately and said he was at the cottage and would love to meet Marion. Erin explained that Marion had heard the recording of his story and been quite emotional. She suggested they bring her to the cottage that morning. Curtis explained he had taken Carl and Kyle to the airport for the early flight, and had just returned when her call came.

Erin passed on the information to Marion, and they offered to take her to the cottage whenever she was ready. Lisa said that they would take her there, but just as far as the cottage. They would do some sightseeing and Marion could then ring them when she wanted picked up.

A short time later, they deposited a nervous Marion at the bottom of the path and drove off. They didn't see the front door open or what happened next.

CHAPTER 11

Marion walked up the path and stopped in front of Curtis. They stared at each other for a few moments, then he moved slowly towards her. 'What happens now?' he asked quietly.

Suddenly, Marion rushed forward and threw herself into his arms. Their embrace lasted for several minutes, then they kissed.

* * * * * *

The girls were parked at a headland when Erin's phone rang. The call came from Curtis.

'Marion and I are reunited, but she is too emotional to talk to you. She plans to contact Joseph later and arrange a meeting. We're not sure how that will work out, but thanks for all your help.'

Erin and Lisa continued their sightseeing before returning their hired car. Back in the hotel, they had lunch before packing and taking a taxi to the airport.

* * * * * *

Once more back in Stevenage, Erin hugged Lisa goodbye and the next morning she headed into the family depot. Her dad was delighted to see her and wanted to hear all about her trip.

'Would you call Uncle Eric, please, and ask him to come through to your office?' she asked. 'I have a story to tell.'

No more work took place that morning as Erin related her meeting with her long-lost Uncle Curtis, and together they listened to the recording.

'Wow! Wow! Wow!' exclaimed James, looking at Eric. 'What do we do now?'

Erin broke in before Eric answered, and told them of Curtis and Marion's reunion.

'I'm looking forward to hearing how the meeting with Joseph went,' she added.

'We will wait to hear about that,' said Eric, 'and if all is well, we need to plan a reunion. We can shut up shop for a week and take a family holiday in Jersey. You won't mind coming again, would you, Erin?'

'Try and stop me,' she laughed.

* * * * * *

The following day, at work, Erin's phone rang. She immediately recognised Marion's number.

After exchanging pleasantries for a few moments, Erin waited to hear Marion's news.

'Well,' began the older woman, 'two things to report. The meeting with Curtis and Joseph, and indeed my dad, went well. The second bit of news is that Curtis and I are getting married. So, please accept an invitation to our June wedding.'

'That is wonderful news,' replied Erin, and relayed the plans for a family reunion.

'Well,' laughed Marion, 'why not make it the week of the wedding? 30th of June is our date. Curtis is holding onto the cottage for now, and hoping to get a job with his old company. That's as far as the plans go meanwhile. I'll be in touch.'

Erin told her dad and Uncle Eric the news, and the week of 26th June to 3rd July was decided as the planned family holiday. Erin rang and told Lisa, who said she would talk to her boss and, if necessary, take unpaid leave.

For Erin, the next few weeks seemed to crawl by, but eventually, the time for the holiday arrived. Eric had booked plane tickets, including one for Lisa who didn't have to take unpaid leave. He also booked the *Pomme d'Or* Hotel again as a party booking. Not all of the family could come, but Eric and Cynthia, James, Grace, Erin and Lisa made up the travelling party.

The warm Jersey sun greeted them as they stepped off the plane, and waiting in the reception were Curtis, Marion, and Joseph. Tear-filled hugs followed as the brothers were reunited, and only Joseph, Erin, and Lisa managed to control their emotions. Curtis had hired a minibus to transport everyone to the hotel, where he had booked dinner.

They chatted through the meal then, with more hugs, Marion, Curtis, and Joseph said their goodbyes.

'See you at the wedding,' Curtis told them. 'And enjoy seeing around the old homeland.'

* * * * * *

Before the wedding, Eric had talked on the phone to Curtis and Marion and persuaded them to let him host the reception at the *Pomme d'Or*. Curtis told Eric that they were having a Registry Office wedding and asked him to stand as a witness, alongside Marion's schoolteacher friend Sharon.

Marion had decided she would dress formally for the occasion, though not in a wedding, but she wanted the men to wear morning suits.

'This girl,' Curtis told his brother, 'knows what she wants.' He told Eric that they could hire their suits and gave him the address of a tailor in St Helier where he could go to be measured up.

* * * * * *

On the day of the wedding, everyone arrived at the Registry Office, dressed in their chosen outfits. Along with the close family, there were a few other friends of the bride and groom.

As Curtis and Eric stood before the Registrar, awaiting the arrival of the bride, Joseph hit the button on his stereo player and the sound of Seal singing *Kiss from a Rose* accompanied Marion, her dad, and Sharon as they walked towards the front of the room. Marion wore a high-necked, below-the-knee pink dress, and carried a simple bouquet of flowers. Sharon wore a traditional bridesmaid's dress in blue, and Marion's dad looked the part in his morning suit and buttonhole.

The simple ceremony itself took very little time, with no religious content allowed, and Shania Twain's *From This Moment On* entertained the congregation during the signing of the register and continued as the entourage walked to the waiting car. Although the reception venue was within walking distance, Eric had insisted on the happy couple taking a car ride around the town while the guests assembled at the hotel.

When they eventually arrived, a photographer took several photos before everyone assembled in The Wharfe Suite for the reception. And after a delicious meal, Eric, Curtis, and Dan made short but relevant speeches, and finally Joseph made an emotional tribute to his mum and new-found dad.

Eric had arranged for the entire wedding party to spend the night in the hotel, with the bridge and groom staying in the Bridal Suite. And the following morning everyone got together for breakfast. Then they assembled in the foyer to wave Marion and Curtis off on their honeymoon – a trip to Austria.

* * * * * *

On the Sunday following the wedding, the family hired a seven-seater vehicle and, with Erin guiding, visited the former home of Eric, Joseph, and Curtis. They spent some time exploring before stopping at the *Bon Nuit* Café for lunch. Joseph, now back at work, looked after their requirements.

Before they left, he sought Erin out.

'Lovely meeting you, my dear cousin,' he said. 'I'll say goodbye,' and he hugged her before adding, 'but I think you are a Jersey girl, and you will be back.'

* * * * * *

The next day, the family and Lisa headed in two taxis to the airport. As the plane lifted into the blue Jersey sky, Erin looked back at the retreating Island and smiled to herself.

Jersey girl? I don't know, she thought. *I'm happy to have been here and part of this adventure, but glad to be going home.*

The Incident at
the Horse's Heads

CHAPTER 1

My name is Philip Robinson, and I am a Detective Police Sergeant. Vivian, my wife, and I had driven through the round-about sporting two wired horses' heads on several occasions, always on our way to Donegal.

But on this particular day, an incident occurred which led not only to a traffic jam, but an abduction.

I heard the crash and climbed from my car in time to see a man get out of a black car which had crashed with force into the rear of a red car. But it soon appeared he was not there to assist the occupants of the red car. Instead, he pulled the girl passenger from the vehicle and began to drag her towards another black car which was sitting in an approach road.

By this time, I was running towards the scene and flashed my badge, shouting, 'Stop, police!'

But by the time I got closer, the abductor had bundled the girl into the waiting vehicle, and it spun round with its rear doors still open and screeched off in the direction of the app-roach road.

I memorised the number and quickly jotted it down as I retraced my steps to the red car.

By this time, other motorists were gathering. I showed my badge and asked everyone to stay clear, that this was now a crime scene, then phoned 999 and explained who I was and demanded an ambulance and police. I asked the onlookers to return to their cars and wait.

When I reached the crashed red car, I looked in through the open door and saw a badly shaken lady driver. Vivian appeared and climbed in beside her, taking the woman's hand to reassure her, and explained that the police and an ambulance were on their way. Vivian had been a police officer herself many years before but, following an accident while on duty, had retired on medical grounds.

A few minutes later, two police cars arrived, closely followed by an ambulance. The paramedics took over from Vivian while I spoke to the police officer in charge. Meanwhile, other constables directed the queue of traffic. I assured my colleague I would give a written report into the local station, then Vivian and I returned to our car.

However, instead of heading towards Donegal, I drove to the police station in Strand Road. The desk sergeant was expecting us, so Vivian and I were made comfortable and I wrote out my report. I gave the signed statement to the sergeant, then we left.

Using a different route than originally planned, we resumed our journey to Donegal, and an hour and a half later, we settled into our Downing's caravan.

Although I was on a week's break, I kept in touch with my colleagues and learned that the driver of the red car – Mrs Joan Murray – had identified the abductor as her passenger's estranged husband.

Records showed that he had recently secured his release from prison following a two-year sentence for drugs offences. Before going to jail, the passenger, Clare, had told him she didn't want him to have anything more to do with her or their children. And she had moved away from their home to settle in another district, well away from Derry.

Joan Murray had told my colleagues that she felt the abduction was her fault.

She explained, 'I persuaded Clare to come on a weekend break with me, but to stay at my home overnight before departure. One of my neighbours must have recognised Clare and somehow got word to her husband, or one of his friends.'

I also learned that the two black cars involved in the incident had been stolen the night before from a dealer's forecourt in Buncrana. The second car had turned up abandoned and burned-out on waste ground in Letterkenny.

* * * * * *

Knowing that this would now be a Garda case, I relaxed to enjoy my break. On day two, while Vivian and I were having breakfast, we heard a car pull up. A minute later, there was a knock on our caravan door.

I opened the door and immediately recognised the face of the man in the Garda uniform. Jim Boyd, an old mate from my shirt factory days, stood on the deck.

'Hello, mucker,' he greeted me.

I invited him in and introduced him to Vivian, who was still in her dressing gown. She quickly excused herself.

'I hope you don't mind me calling so early,' began Jim, 'but I rang the station asking to speak to the officer on the scene of the crash last Thursday, and they gave me your name. I knew you had joined the police force after leaving the factory, but you could have knocked me down with a feather when I discovered that you were the one I wanted to speak with.'

'How can I help you, friend?' I asked.

'We know the abductor,' replied Jim. 'He's a drug pusher just out of prison, but I wonder if you managed to get a good look at the driver of the getaway car?'

'I did,' I replied, 'but he is not in our books.'

'Yes, so your station said,' confirmed Jim. 'However, I thought maybe you could come to our station and look at some mugshots. One never knows, you might spot him.'

'Will do,' I said. 'Vivian is going shopping with our next-door neighbour this morning, so I am at a loose end.'

When Vivian returned, fully dressed for her outing, I explained what Jim wanted and followed him to his car.

'I hope my neighbours don't think you are arresting me,' I said with a laugh.

Jim smiled, started the car, and deliberately drove around the circular site before exiting.

'That will give them something to talk about,' he remarked with a laugh.

At the Garda Station, Jim sat me down in front of a computer screen then touched a button and photographs appeared. After 15 minutes, my eyes were growing bleary, when a figure appeared and I called to stop.

'This face looks familiar,' I said, 'but I don't suppose you have a picture of the back of his head?'

Jim smiled. 'No, why?'

'As the car turned,' I explained, 'I saw the back of his head. And why are you smiling?'

'No, go on, Phil.'

'Well, it could have been a trick of the light,' I continued, 'but I could see the figure's dark hair, and down the back there seemed to be a triangular bald patch.'

'That's why I'm smiling,' said Jim. 'I just knew you had got him in one.'

I looked up at him enquiringly.

'In prison, he made some enemies. And one day, as he collected shirts from the laundry, another prisoner rushed at him, brandishing a hot iron. Before the officer could reach them, the assailant had slammed the iron down on our friend here's head.' He pointed at the photograph on the screen. 'In the hospital, he had to have a skin graft and, of course, his hair never grew back. Well done, Phil!'

I rose, and we shook hands. 'I will have someone drive you back, and thanks once again,' said Jim.

He called over a young Garda officer and instructed him to drive me to my caravan.

I never saw Jim again, but attended his funeral. He was shot in the line of duty while attempting to arrest a black-haired man — a man with a skin patch on the back of his head.

Jim's colleagues told me that the abductor husband had been found and arrested, and his wife safely reunited with her children.

* * * * * *

Vivian and I continue to go to our caravan, but we never pass through the horses' heads roundabout without remembering the day of the 'Incident at Horses' Heads'.

The Wind Bloweth Where it Listeth'

CHAPTER 1

Margaret lay in her bed and listened as the wind howled around the house. She then heard it rattle above her head in the roof space.

An old Bible verse came into her mind. 'The wind bloweth where it listeth.' She reached for her MacBook Air laptop and tapped in her password, then the word listeth – pleases.

Another loud brattle from above, and Margaret said to herself, 'You certainly blow where you please.'

Another thought entered her head that pigs can see the wind. 'How terrible,' she said out loud. Suddenly, there was another even louder rattle and cracking sound from above, and her ceiling split.

Margaret rose and dressed. As she packed her laptop, brush, comb, and make-up into her knapsack, her bedroom door opened. Her father, James, stood there fully dressed.

'Oh, good, you're dressed. I'm afraid the old house is under attack, and the storm is getting worse. The river has just burst its banks and the water is running down the streets.'

Her young sister, Lucy, now also dressed, appeared in the doorway crying, 'Part of my roof fell in on my bed.'

'We'd better pack what we can and go,' said Dad, just as another part of Margaret's ceiling cracked and then collapsed. She looked up and could see the night sky, then felt the rain.

Quickly, the family began packing clothes into suitcases which Margaret and her father carried downstairs. Water was already gushing under the front door and flooding across the hallway.

'Wait here,' shouted James, and donned his raincoat. As he opened the front door, more water gushed in; already it was up to his knees. After a few minutes, his car appeared outside.

He rushed upstairs and grabbed the two cases they had managed to pack, then waded back to the car and put the luggage in the boot. He then grabbed coats from the coat rack and threw them in on top of the cases. Back at the top of the stairs, he brought his wife Jane from their bedroom, and gently led her down the stairs. Then, like a hero from a novel, he picked her up and carried her to the car.

Margaret told Lucy to wait, and she ran downstairs and waded after her dad to open the car door. Even as he placed Jane inside, the water followed. He hastily closed the door as Margaret appeared, carrying a stricken Lucy. The fierce wind whipped the water into waves as they managed to get into the rear seats.

As James finally drove slowly away, roof tiles flew down into the rapidly rising water. After about a hundred metres, the car engine stuttered to a stop, and the family now sat marooned.

Just then three firemen appeared, dragging a rubber lifeboat. Opening the car doors, they helped the four passengers out and into the raft. Slowly they pushed and pulled the lifeboat through the flood, while almost losing their balance in the strong wind. Eventually, they reached the bottom of Blair Hill and tied the boat to the railings while they helped the family out and told them to make their way up the slope.

Other figures appeared to help, and together everyone struggled up the hill to the grounds of the Secondary School and then into its foyer. As two helpers closed large doors against the almost prevailing wind, James, Jane, Margaret, and Lucy were led through the school and into the sports hall.

About 40 other villagers were already there, seated on sports mats. Wet and cold, Margaret and her family huddled in a corner. Blankets were brought out by teachers and youth club leaders who Margaret recognised. They also brought towels, and showed Jane the changing rooms, suggesting she go and take off her wet clothes. Margaret went with her mum while James helped Lucy out of her clothes and wrapped her in a blanket. She felt too damp and cold to be modest.

Later, wrapped in blankets and towels, the family sat down together on the mats.

A figure approached who Margaret recognised as George Kirby, the school principal.

'Hello, James,' he greeted. He knew Margaret's dad from the bowling club. 'Glad you made it. I've just had word that the whole village on both sides of the river is... a river. The water level has reached windowsill height.'

More wind whistled down the school corridors as three more families entered the sports hall.

A young woman with an elderly woman entered, followed by a young man carrying blankets and towels. The woman gathered two rugs in her arms and guided the elderly lady towards the toilets.

Margaret had draped her trousers and jumper on a radiator in the changing room, and she went in to check on them. Thinking they were dry enough, she entered a cubicle to dress then returned to the sports hall and headed to a table located near the stage with tea and coffee thermal pump containers to provide hot drinks.

She poured two cups of tea, added a little milk, and took them to her parents. Then she went back to the table and poured out a glass of orange squash for Lucy, and took a plate with a few biscuits to her. Finally, she returned to the table to pour herself a cup of coffee, just as the young man she had seen earlier joined her.

'Hello,' he said. 'I think my sister knows you. Would you like to come over?'

'Yes, of course,' replied Margaret. And carrying their coffees, they walked to where his group were seated.

The young woman looked up. 'Margaret Wilkes?'

'That's me,' responded Margaret, 'and you are Jennifer Steel. I recognise you now.'

'Well, Jennifer Lynch now,' she said. 'My husband is in Germany with his work and trying to get to us as quickly as possible. This is my mum, and my elder brother Jon. He's an accountant in Nottingham.'

'I was just on a visit to see Mum,' Jon explained, 'when the storm hit.'

After a brief chat, Margaret noticed that Jon had Wi-Fi.

'How did you manage that?' she asked.

'The Principal let me into his office, and I reset the router,' he explained. 'Here's the password.'

He showed Margaret the router password which she copied to her phone.

'Thanks,' she said. 'I must get back to my family.'

Once more back in her corner, Margaret pulled her MacBook Air laptop from her holdall and entered her password, followed by the password for the router.

'Ah, success,' she said out loud, and passed the information on to her dad.

CHAPTER 2

James Wilkes worked for an accountancy firm in York, but chose to live in the small village of
Sheephaven. He had purchased the cottage they lived in as an investment before he married, and had lived there as a young man during part of each summer, preferring the city life for the rest of the year. When he met and married Jane, she had fallen in love with the cottage, and they moved their permanently when Margaret was born. Lucy arrived as a surprise many years later.

Jane had worked as a hairdresser in the village until she contracted Parkinson's.

Margaret had studied law and gained her experience with the law firm of Carrington and Kerr in York. Just two years after Lucy's birth, she sat and passed her Bar Exam. But her mother's Parkinson's struck the day of Lucy's second birthday, when James and Margaret both noticed her difficulty lighting the candles and failure to cut the cake.

As a junior in the law firm, Margaret enjoyed her work, but she resigned to look after mother as the Parkinson's progressed.

A week before the fateful storm, Margaret had had a surprise visit from her ex-boss Bill Carrington. He wanted to enquire after the family and to see if Margaret could return to the practice, even on a part-time basis. She had said she would give it some thought, and her dad had persuaded her to say yes when the storm arrived.

* * * * * *

Few people slept that night. And as daylight filtered into the school hall, Jon approached Margaret to say that although the wind had abated, the water levels were still high.

James left his group and walked to the bottom of the hill. He removed his shoes and socks, rolled up his trousers above his knees and, using the footpath, waded through the now knee-high water towards his house. He passed his car – still waterlogged above the level of the car seats – and eventually reached the cottage.

The family home looked a sorry sight. Many of the roof tiles had blown off, and the water had created a lot of damage inside. James moved through the cottage to the rear store where he retrieved his fisherman's waders from the cupboard. Climbing a few flights of stairs, he rolled down his trouser legs. After replacing his socks, he put his shoes in his pockets and pulled on the waders.

Now waterproofed, James waded to his car and opened the boot. He then threw the coats over his shoulder, removed the cases, and made his way back towards the school. Once inside, James removed his waders – with Jon's help – and replaced his shoes. Then the two men carried the cases and coats to the Wilkes family corner and explained how he managed his task.

In a short while, the family were clothed and ready for James's next plan. He had earlier Googled a map of the district and discovered that Blair Hill connected to a 'B' road, which in turn connected the 'A' road leading into York – a distance of just over two miles. James waited until after 8am and then phoned a taxi firm he sometimes used, and spoke with the receptionist. He identified himself and asked about the weather conditions. Told that things had settled down in the area, he explained his circumstances, he asked if the firm would send a taxi via the A and B roads to Blair Hill and into the Blair Hill Secondary School car park.

The receptionist said she would check with the boss and ring James back. He then made another phone call and booked two rooms at the Royal Hotel in York.

A few minutes later, James's phone rang.

'Hi James,' said the caller, 'Mike here. I believe you have had flooding problems.'

'Hi Mike,' James replied. 'Yes, the house is a mess, and the village still flooded. So, can you help me?'

'No problem,' responded Mike. 'I'll send a taxi via the back roads. How many passengers?'

'Four,' replied James, 'and as soon as you can, Mike, thanks.'

James stood at the door to wait, and when the taxi arrived he gathered up his family and luggage and said goodbye to the remaining evacuees.

The cabbie made his way through various twisting roads to the main road and then on to the Royal Hotel in York, where he helped to unload the luggage and carry the cases into the foyer. James paid the fare with a substantial tip and checked in at the hotel reception for an indefinite period.

Once they had taken their cases and coats to the adjacent rooms, the family went for breakfast, then all except James went back upstairs to sleep. In the meantime, James made several phone calls. One was to his firm, to explain his situation and to ask for his workload to be transferred to his computer. The next calls were to his house insurance and car insurance companies, acquainting them of the circumstances and damage to both cottage and car. He then went upstairs and, exhausted, snuggled in beside Jane and slept.

* * * * * *

Later that day, James persuaded Margaret to go back to work, saying he could work from his hotel room.

And when Margaret turned up the following morning, Mr Carrington showed his delight by lifting and swinging her around. The rest of the staff were delighted to see her, and it didn't take Margaret long to get back into the swing of things, as she informed Mr Carrington with a laugh.

CHAPTER 3

The family stayed in the hotel for a week before James found and rented an apartment in York. It meant, of course, Lucy had to start at a new school, as her old school had been badly damaged in the storm and would take quite a while to be assessed and repaired. Meanwhile, James had his car recovered, repaired and delivered to his new address. The water had drained away from the village streets, and work had begun on repairs to the cottage.

Margaret retrieved her undamaged car from the incline beside the cottage, and slowly, life returned to a sense of normality.

* * * * * *

Months passed before the family returned to inspect the renovated cottage. Jane stopped at the door, shook her head furiously, and refused to enter. Margaret took her back to the car, where she said she would wait.

Margaret joined her dad and Lucy in the hallway, and they walked from room to room, then upstairs. The repairs were excellent, and the cottage looked better than new.

'I don't think you'll get Mum back in here, Dad,' said Margaret.

'No, nor me,' Lucy retorted. 'Anyway, I like my new school, Dad.'

James looked from Lucy to Margaret. 'And you?' he asked.

She shrugged. 'If Mum won't come back, Dad, then neither will I. Sorry,' Margaret replied.

'In that case,' James sighed, 'I'll put the cottage on the market. We'll stay in the apartment and, when it sells, I'll... no, we'll look for somewhere new in York or nearby.'

Lucy and Margaret hugged him, and all three returned to the car. James told Margaret their plans, which brought a radiant smile to her face.

* * * * * *

James waited until the next spring until the work in the village was complete before putting the cottage on the market. And although it took until August to sell, it eventually did for a good price. James and Margaret visited several estate agents and scoured the ads in the local papers and eventually, after looking at several houses, found one which both felt suited their needs. It pleased even Lucy and Jane, whose health had continued to deteriorate.

The large four-bedroomed bungalow stood in a beautiful location on the outskirts of the city of York, and the owners accepted their offer. So, the family moved in at the beginning of September, just in time for Lucy to start her Autumn term.

Margaret and Jon had kept in touch via Facebook messenger, and one day she announced that he was planning to visit. He arrived the following week and stayed for a few days in the spare room, which doubled as James's office.

It came as no surprise when, after many similar visits, he had an important conversation with James. And the following day, he and Margaret announced their engagement.

This announcement, of course, delighted Jane and Lucy, who immediately announced she wanted to be a bridesmaid.

Margaret and Jon had met up with Jon's sister, mother and family during the previous months, so everyone knew of their intentions. Unfortunately, three weeks before the planned Spring wedding, Jon's mother died.

Jon and Margaret married in April on a beautiful sunny day. Jane attended in a wheelchair, Lucy fulfilled her role as bridesmaid, Jon's friend from work stood as best man, and the whole day went splendidly. Then the happy couple headed off to honeymoon in Crete.

For a few months after the wedding, Margaret and Jon lived almost separate lives until Jon's firm finally opened an office in York, which had been on the cards for some time, and he transferred to manage it. He and Margaret purchased an apartment in York, and finally, their lives became 'married bliss'.

* * * * * *

In September of the following year, Lucy became an aunty.

Sand, Sea and Adventure

CHAPTER 1

Phew, it is hot!' said Marcus to no-one in particular. But his companions responded. "That's why we're here, Marcus,' said Geoff.

"Why we're here,' echoed Artie.

"Too hot for me,' said Marcus. 'I'm going for a swim. Are you coming?'

'You go ahead,' replied Geoff. 'I'll join you shortly.'

With that, Marcus discarded his sandshoes and trotted towards the sea.

Marcus loved the clear blue ocean, and dived and surfaced and dived. Suddenly, as he surfaced, something struck him on the head and then on his body. Marcus felt himself being dragged through the water until he managed to push the offending object aside. Although racked with pain, Marcus tried to swim, spurred on by adrenalin. But eventually, exhausted, he turned on his back and floated. Bit by bit, the outgoing tide swept the now unconscious Marcus further out to sea.

* * * * * *

Geoff woke with a start. 'Goodness, I slept.' His eyes stung and his body was covered in sand.

He sat up and took his watch from the pocket of his shorts. It was 20 minutes since Marcus had left to go swimming. Geoff sat up and looked at the orange haze covering the beach. The sea had disappeared in the haze, and people were running along the beach from the sea.

'Artie! Artie!' he called to his pal, who had also fallen asleep. 'I can't see Marcus.'

Geoff and Artie scrambled up from their beach towels and ran to the seashore. They split up, and Geoff walked one way while Artie headed in the opposite direction, the sand stinging their faces. They met up again, their eyes streaming, their breathing restricted; neither had caught sight of Marcus.

They staggered up the beach to the shelter of the promenade hut, where they washed their eyes and faces in the drinking fountains. Next, the two friends made their way to the Beachside Hotel, where they joined the crowd of other residents waiting for the lifts and climbing the stairs. Using the stairways to the second floor, Geoff and Artie entered their room and took turns to shower.

Marcus's clothes were still laid out on his bed, which showed that he had not returned.

Through the window, all the two room-mates could see was the deepening orange haze. They had heard of Sahara sandstorms affecting the Canary Islands before, but in all the years they had come to Tenerife for Winter sun, they had never experienced one.

Driven by the wind, the sand had taken the islanders and holidaymakers by surprise.

Geoff rang the hotel reception and explained the situation regarding Marcus. The receptionist said that she would inform both the beach patrol and the coastguard.

The coastguard had already reported a rescue at 11.30, when a jet-skier fell off his machine. The man had eventually managed to catch it, and tried in vain to climb aboard. In the end, exhausted, he managed to just cling on and remove his waterproof phone from the pocket of his wetsuit, to dial the emergency number. The lifeboat rescued him and his jet-ski within minutes, floating a kilometre or so from the shore.

Following Geoff's alert, the lifeboat searched the area again, but the sudden sandstorm hampered their search and the crew found no sign of Marcus.

CHAPTER 2

A corpse will usually float face-down in the water. But Marcus was alive and, although unconscious, floated on his back. When consciousness slowly returned, he found himself enshrouded in an orange mist, his mouth filled with sand. Turning on his face, he rinsed his mouth and nose out in the saltwater.

His head and body ached, and his throat felt parched. Once again, he turned on his back and floated, but all he could see through smarting eyes was the orange mist.

Suddenly, he felt strong hands dragging him from the water, then he again lost consciousness.

Some time later, when he opened his eyes, he saw a face peer into his and heard a distant voice speak in Spanish. 'Hola. Hola.'

Through parched lips, Marcus responded, 'Hello.'

'Ah, English,' said the voice. And the face disappeared.

A short while later another face appeared, and another voice spoke. 'Hello, how are you?'

The person lying on the bed croaked, 'I don't know.'

'Who are you?' The voice asked as the face became clearer.

'I don't know!' came the reply. 'Where am I?'

'You are in hospital in Madeira,' came the reply. 'A fishing boat on the way to Spain picked you out of the water. And the crew left you here. You have been severely injured and drifting in and out of consciousness. You have several broken ribs and a fractured skull.' The man went on, 'I am a hospital consultant, Mr Martinez. And you?'

'I... I can't remember,' the patient said, before once again lapsing into an unconscious state.

* * * * *

Back in the Puerto de la Cruz resort of Tenerife, Geoff and Artie awaited reports from the coastguards and police. No-one had seen or found out anything about Marcus. The searchers concluded that he must have drowned and his body swept out to sea.

For Geoff and Artie, the holiday had ended. They packed their cases and Marcus's, and prepared for home as soon as they could arrange flights. Meanwhile, Geoff phoned Marcus's parents and his girlfriend, and broke the sad news. He assured them he would let them know of any future developments.

By the time they left for their flights to leave Tenerife, Geoff and Artie had received no more updates on Marcus.

******

'How's Jason Bourne?' A junior doctor, Ramon, asked the consultant.

'I beg your pardon?' Martinez replied.

'Your memory loss patient,' the young doctor responded in their native Portuguese.

'I'm not with you,' replied Mr Martinez, and walked away.

Earlier in the canteen, the young doctor and a colleague had joked that the patient's situation was similar to that of the fictional Jason Bourne in *The Bourne Identity* – a film the consultant had not seen.

In the film, a man had been pulled out of the water by fishermen, having been shot and suffering memory loss. The memory loss is where the similarity ended, but the name Jason stuck among the staff.

Phone calls to the police in England regarding the patient had drawn a blank. The pick-up point suggested he might have drifted from Spain, but from there too there was nothing.

Weeks passed into months. 'Jason' had been transferred to a private ward on government funds, and in Tenerife, the story of Marcus had faded into obscurity. The sandstorm damage had quickly been cleared away, and holidaymakers had returned for the late Spring sunshine.

One morning, a clerk at the Puerto de la Cruz hotel was given the task of checking through the names and address of guests who had stayed there during the sandstorm incident. The management had decided to write and offer them a further holiday at a reduced rate.

Suddenly, a name struck a chord, Marcus Williams. The clerk had been on duty the day this chap had disappeared, presumed drowned. He contacted his superiors, who transferred the name and UK address to the police.

At the station, Police Officer Adriano looked through the record of the events and asked to see his Commissioner. He took along a copy of the document to the Commissioner's office. Commissioner Alfredo glanced at the report, then said, 'Well?'

'Sir, this young man had been swimming close to where another incident occurred. A jet-skier reported striking a submerged rock which knocked him off his jet-ski.'

'So?' enquired his superior.

'Well, sir,' continued Adriano, 'I scuba dived all along that range of the coast. There are no submerged rocks anywhere in that area. What if the jet-ski had struck this lad Marcus?'

'Then maybe dragged him to where they found the jet-ski?' his superior surmised.

'That was during the sandstorm,' continued the officer, 'and there was a powerful wind at that time. His body could have drifted a good distance from our island.'

'But to where?' asked the Commissioner, looking at his wall map.

'To Madeira!' their voices cried together.

'Worth a try,' said the Commissioner. 'Things are quiet, so go ahead and call the officers there. But remember, they speak Portuguese.'

* * * * * *

In the Funchal police station, the telephone rang. In Portuguese, the desk officer answered, 'Hello. Officer Barboza.'

The caller, also in Portuguese, replied, 'Good morning, my name is Alberto Garcia, and I am a police officer with the Tenerife Force.' Adriano knew his colleague Alberto spoke several languages, including Portuguese, so had asked him to help.

'I am going to ask what may be a silly question,' said Alberto, 'but did you have a body wash up on your shores lately?'

The Funchal officer laughed. 'No, but we had a live one delivered to us several weeks ago. Why do you ask?'

Alberto replied, 'We had a young Englishman go missing at sea during the sandstorm, and his name has come to our attention again.'

'This guy came to us,' continued Officer Barboza, 'badly injured and picked up by a Spanish fishing vessel. But he has amnesia and is still recovering in hospital.'

'I know it's a long shot,' said Alberto, 'but if I send you a photograph of our missing person, would you check?'

'Of course,' replied Barboza. 'Go ahead.'

The Police Commissioner and Officer Adriano had sat nearby during the conversation, and Alberto now turned to them and repeated what had been said.

'Ok,' said the Commissioner, 'a long shot it may be, but get in touch with this guy's family and have them send us a recent photo.'

Once again, Alberto had the task of making contact. But Marcus's mobile number was the only one he had, so he tried that.

A surprised young voice answered, 'Hello.'

Alberto introduced himself and stated the reason for his call, but without going into details.

The person on the mobile identified herself as Marcus's girlfriend Veronica; she explained that his family had passed the mobile phone on to her, after his friend Geoff had brought it back from Tenerife.

Veronica offered to send a fairly recent photo of her and Marcus, and passed on her contact details. Alberto gave her the station's email address and thanked her for her help.

Once again Alberto relayed the conversation to the other two officers, and five minutes later the computer alerted them to an incoming message, and the scanned photo of Marcus appeared.

Alberto emailed the photo to the Funchal police station computer, and they awaited a reply.

Within minutes, Officer Barboza called to acknowledge receipt of the picture and said he would have it delivered to the hospital with an explanation along with the Tenerife station's phone number.

Later that afternoon, the station phone rang and a caller asked in Portuguese to speak to Alberto. The man explained that he was Consultant Carlos Martinez and confirmed that, although his patient had received several severe injuries, it would appear that he and the man in the photo were the same.

Alberto suggested that Dr Martinez should get in touch with Marcus's girlfriend, Veronica and gave him her contact details, explaining that she could perhaps provide some answers.

CHAPTER 3

Vera Williams, Marcus's widowed mother, lived in Cirencester, a market town in Gloucestershire, around 80 miles west of London. That evening, she received a visit from her missing son's girlfriend, Veronica, who related the conversations she'd had with first the police and then the Madeira hospital consultant, Carlos Martinez.

On hearing that her son might still be alive, Vera hugged the girl and cried.

'The hospital requires an insurance document,' Veronica explained.

The two women immediately began to look through Marcus's belongings, which Geoff had brought back from Tenerife. In his knapsack, Veronica uncovered the travel insurance documents and suggested that the two women should travel to Madeira to check if the person was Marcus.

* * * * * *

A few days later, with flight and hotel arrangements made, Veronica and Vera flew to Madeira, where the younger woman hired a car and drove them to their hotel. Once checked in, they immediately headed to the hospital, where Veronica asked to see the consultant, Carlos Martinez. After a short wait, the man arrived.

He shook hands with both ladies. 'Good, you caught me in a quiet period. Come this way.'

He led them to the ward where the patient known only as 'Jason' slept.

'As you can see,' Carlos pointed out, 'he had some bad injuries, thought they have mostly cleared up now. But he sleeps a lot.'

He gently shook the patient. 'Marcus,' he said, using the young man's real name.

Marcus opened his eyes and stared at his visitors.

'Hello, son,' said Vera.

Marcus closed his eyes for quite a while before letting out a long sigh. He then put his hands to his head and groaned.

'Where on earth's face am I?' Then he opened his eyes and smiled. ' Mum, and Veronica!' he exclaimed. 'What happened?'

The two women rushed to his bedside and clasped his hands. He then reached up and hugged them both. Tears flowed from all three, then Marcus fell back on his bed exhausted, breathing heavily and gasping.

Carlos drew the ladies back and ushered them to chairs at the side of the bed.

'Give him a while,' he suggested. Then he asked. 'Did you bring any documents?'

Veronica opened her bag and handed over Marcus's travel insurance documents and his passport.

'Thank you,' said Carlos, smiling. 'Well, you certainly brought him back to reality. Wait here. He will come round again shortly, but don't tell him too much at once. I will go and formalize these documents.'

* * * * * *

After a while, Marcus's breathing eased, and he opened his eyes.

'Oh,' he said, frowning, 'so many flashing memories of sand, sea, and faces.' He struggled to a sitting position. 'What happened, and where am I?'

Vera said, 'We are not to tell you too much at once. Sufficient to say you had an accident on holiday and ended up in a hospital on the island of Madeira.'

'We flew out today,' Veronica explained, 'and our faces seemed to jog your memory.'

Once again, Marcus fell back on his pillows. 'I feel exhausted.'

'Look,' said his mother, 'you rest, and we will go and speak to the doctor. Anyway, I need a cup of tea.' She smiled, leaned forward, and kissed him. Veronica squeezed his hand, and gently kissed the boyfriend she thought she had lost. Marcus was already asleep when they left the room.

The two women asked the way to the Consultant's office, and a lady brought them tea and biscuits.

'I have talked with the insurance company and explained the situation,' said Carlos. 'They explained that everything must be paid for by Marcus and then reclaimed from the company. They saw no problem, but,' he frowned, 'I'm afraid the bill is horrendous.'

'There is no such thing as horrendous,' responded Vera, 'now that I have my son back.'

* * * * * *

Later, back in the ward, they sat and talked with Marcus. He remembered a little of being with Geoff and Artie but nothing of his accident.

'No-one here knows what happened,' said Veronica, 'except that a fishing vessel picked you up from the sea and brought you here.'

Marcus laughed. 'That's why they called me Jason.'

'Pardon?' Vera looked confused.

'Ah!' Veronica laughed. 'Jason Bourne!'

Marcus nodded as a perplexed Vera looked from one to another. Before they could explain, there was a knock at the door and Doctor Ramon peered into the room.

'Hello,' he said in heavily accented English. ' Hi, Jason, I hear you now have your own name.' He came closer to the bed and shook Marcus's hand.

'Let me explain,' said Veronica to a still perplexed Vera.

She explained the story of the fictitious Jason Bourne and his rescue from the sea, and how something similar happened to Marcus. She then introduced herself and Vera to Ramon, who bowed, waved to Marcus, and left.

As he left, Carlos entered the ward. 'Ladies, I have good and bad news for you. First, the bad news. Marcus will have to stay another few days before we can let you take him home. Now, the good news. A Government official is coming to speak with you regarding help with the finances. He will call here tomorrow afternoon at two o'clock, and we will meet in my office. That's all I can tell you.'

* * * * * *

After an early and hearty breakfast, Vera and Veronica drove to the hospital where they spent the morning with Marcus before leaving for a brief walk in the fresh air ahead of their meeting.

At ten to two, they presented themselves at the Consultant's office and waited for the Government official. He arrived just after two o'clock and, after introductions, got straight down to business.

With Carlos interpreting, the man explained, 'Following a meeting in Government House and a discussion on the miraculous survival of the patient, our Government decided to help you regarding the cost of the patient's treatment.

'The total cost came to 25,000 Euros,' Carlos said, 'but the Government has generously agreed to cover one-fifth of the cost.'

Senor Grigori, the official, then produced some forms. 'These are the agreement papers. A copy for you and a copy for me. That is, if you are willing to accept our terms?'

Carlos translated his statement. 'Well, ladies, what do you say? I think it is a very generous offer.'

'Oh,' responded Vera, 'it is more than generous; it is amazing.'

The official spoke again. 'The President of the Regional Government is a very religious man, and he believed that your son's survival could only have been God-granted, and so his proposal to fund part of the financial commitment had been unanimously accepted.'

Again, Carlos translated as the official spoke.

'He is willing for you to sign on behalf of Marcus,' said Carlos, passing two copies of the paperwork to Vera, explaining that one was for her and one for the Government. Vera readily signed even though the document was written in Portuguese and meant nothing to her. The official then signed on behalf of his Government and gave Vera her copy.

With that, he rose, shook both women's hands, bowed to Carlos, and exited the office.

'So,' said Carlos, 'when you can manage it, I require a cheque of the remaining 20,000 Euros, which you can claim from the insurance.'

When he had finished speaking, Veronica reached into her bag and drew out a cheque book. To vera's astonishment, she wrote a cheque for 20,000 euros, tore it out, and handed it to Carlos.

'Close your mouth, Vera,' she said, smiling. ' If you can give me a receipt, Carlos, Marcus can deal with the insurance bit when we get him home.'

Turning to Vera, she explained, 'Marcus and I opened a joint account four years ago and regularly put money into it. We were unofficially engaged and planned to announce it officially and buy a ring when he returned from his holiday with the boys. I didn't want to say anything following his disappearance, as I thought it might just have brought you more grief.'

Vera rose to hug her and sobbed, 'Thank you, dear, for what you've said and done.'

Carlos, who had left the office, returned with an official hospital receipt which he handed to Veronica.

After bringing Marcus up to date, they said goodbye and drove back to the hotel.

Veronica told Vera, 'Because of work commitments, I can't stay any longer, I'm afraid. Will you be all right on your own?'

'Yes,' Vera assured her. 'I contacted Jennifer before we left, and she already offered to come over.' Jennifer was Marcus's sister, who lived with her husband in London. 'She is planning to phone me this evening.'

* * * * * *

The following morning, after a quick visit to say an emotional goodbye to her 'fiancé', Veronica drove to the airport, returned her hired car, and caught her flight home.

She was relieved that Marcus's sister had confirmed she would fly out the following day and join her mother at the hotel.

Arrangements went as planned, and soon Vera and her daughter were sitting beside Marcus in his hospital ward. Marcus admitted that he could remember nothing about the joint account and the secret engagement, but was delighted about the money.

One week later, the hospital discharged Marcus and, in clothes purchased by Jennifer, he joined his mother and sister as they collected their luggage and caught a flight back to London.

EPILOGUE

The wedding of Marcus and Jennifer took place in the September following the homecoming. Geoff was Best Man, and Jennifer Matron of Honour. The insurance company had paid a large portion of the expenses claim.

The miraculous account of Marcus and his deliverance echoed again and again, in the local pub and by Vera's fireside.

The newlyweds, now back working and living in Cirencester, lived 'happily ever after', as all good fairytales end.

And before Marcus junior (although they named him William after his late grandfather) entered the family, a couple of exciting journeys took place. One was to Madeira and one to Tenerife, both of which included happy reunions. Veronica even laughingly agreed on her mother-in-law coming along.

The Mist Aboon the Brae

CHAPTER 1

The three Englishmen stood in the clearing in the Scottish Highlands and groaned as the night descended upon them.

'We may camp here,' said Arthur, the eldest of the three and the leader.

With tents erected, the three men snuggled into their sleeping bags and awaited the dawn.

Even inside his sleeping bag, Billy, the youngest of the three, could feel the Highland air creeping into his bones. He and Gareth shared a tent, while Arthur had one to himself. Eventually, the three adventurers slept.

Next morning, they all seemed to wake at the same time and, clad in their warmest clothes, left their tents to relieve themselves. Arthur lit the camp stove and put oil in the frying pan. Once the fat bubbled, he added three sausages and then broke three eggs into the pan. Gareth lit the other stove and placed a can of water on to boil.

After breakfast and coffee, they peered at their map, decided where they were, and in which direction they would travel.

Dishes washed, packed, tents folded and fastened to their knapsacks, the men prepared for the off. They slung on their backpacks and buckled them into place.

Arthur figured they had walked about a mile from their campsite when they saw the mist descending and settling in the valley below them.

'Brigadoon!' exclaimed Arthur with a laugh. 'Brigadoon.'

Gareth and Billy stared at him.

Billy asked, 'What on earth are you talking about?'

'As a child, my mother took me to see a film in which Gene Kelly and Van Johnson, like us, found themselves lost in the Highlands.'

In storytelling mode, Arthur continued, 'Suddenly, the village of Brigadoon appeared out of the mist. It only appeared once every 100 years and then, only for a day.'

He looked at the expressions on the faces of his companions and laughed. 'Never mind,' he said, 'you're too young. I don't think you'll see Brigadoon today. Come on.'

Still shaking their heads, Gareth and Billy followed Arthur, climbing higher into the hills.

* * * * * *

Arthur and Gareth had met as members of the Solihull Rambler Walking Club. Apart from that, they had little in common.

Arthur had climbed through the ranks of a Birmingham finance company, becoming – at 32 – the youngest CEO to head his department. Gillian had joined the company two years ago as a secretary, and her typing skills and ability to help others in the department led to a swift promotion. When Arthur's PA resigned to take up a position with another company, Margaret Alford, head of secretarial recruitment, recommended Gillian to Arthur. Their professional relationship soon turned personal, with lunch dates, dinner dates, and evenings to the theatre becoming regular occurrences.

Gillian's mum had dementia, and last month, Gillian had surprised Arthur by handing in her notice.

'I need to spend more time looking after Mum,' she had said. 'You met my sister Beth, who is married with three children and lives in Manchester. Beth visits when she can, and we have both noticed Mum's condition worsening. I don't want her going into a home. She raised Beth and I from a young age after our dad died in Afghanistan.'

Arthur remembered Gillian saying that her father had been killed in action as an officer in a tank regiment.

Arthur's own dad had died from a heart attack two years ago, and his mum a month ago, from a stroke. His mother's death had, in a way, prompted this visit to Scotland. While going through her boxes of photos, Arthur had discovered one of a bearded Highlander in Scottish army uniform. The writing on the back of the photo declared him to be Hector MacTavish. He remembered that his grandmother's maiden name had been Jean MacTavish.

Confused why his mother had never mentioned her Scottish connection, he was even more surprised to come across a frayed journal inside an ancient handbag among his mum's possessions.

The journal held his mother's history and explained why she had never discussed it with him. During her teenage years, her family had been involved in smuggling. Most were arrested, hanged, or died in prison; others scattered into the Highlands, and lived and probably died there in obscurity. Arthur's mum had run away to Edinburgh and found work in a factory where she met and married his dad, a carpenter.

Some years later, his father applied for a job with a kitchen manufacturing firm Birmingham. The family was living there when his mum gave birth, as an older first-time mother, to Arthur.

After reading the journal, Arthur had visited Aberdeen and found some of his ancestors' resting places in a local graveyard.

* * * * * *

Gareth, on the other hand, was a victim of redundancy. When he had learned of Arthur's planned trip to Scotland, he'd asked if he could join him. He and his young friend Billy, on a year out from university, had already discussed a hiking holiday before the Summer ended. The idea appealed to Arthur, so the three had made plans for late August.

Gareth, at 24 years of age, still lived with his parents in Solihull. He had worked in a clothing factory which fell foul of cheap imports and, although still operating, now did so with a reduced staff. An employee, since he was 16, Gareth had left with a sizeable redundancy package and intended to look for another job. But not for a while.

* * * * * *

Arthur stopped and pointed. 'Look up ahead, more mist. And this path is getting narrow.'

Suddenly, they heard a young girl's laugh and a figure ran across their path about 50 yards ahead. The three picked up their steps and entered a broad pathway.

Arthur looked to his left. 'That's where she ran. I think we will follow her.'

They had walked about half a mile when, as the mist began to clear, they heard voices and then came upon a campsite.

Two men, sitting by a fire, rose to their feet as Arthur, Gareth and Billy entered.

'Well, hello, hello,' one said in a strong Scottish accent.

'And hello to you,' responded Arthur. 'I'm afraid my friends and I are lost.'

'Never mind,' said the other man. 'Come and sit by the fire and have some refreshments.'

As the two men introduced themselves as brothers, Conor and Hamish MacKay, two women with children emerged from their tents and approached the fire.

CHAPTER 2

Conor introduced them. 'This is my wife, Agnes, and my son Gavin.'

'And,' said Hamish, 'This is Aileen, my wife, and the bonnie wee lassie with her is Alisa, our daughter.'

'I think we heard and glimpsed Alisa earlier, running in the mist,' said Arthur, as the youngster giggled.

Agnes served the visitors coffee. 'I'm giving you nothing to eat,' she said. 'Lunch will be in an hour.'

'That's very generous of you,' Arthur commented.

Turning to her husband, Arthur asked, 'By the way, where are we?'

'You're on the outskirts of Aviemore,' replied Conor. 'We've just come from there and set up camp here.'

'Our campervans,' Hamish joined in, pointing. 'And where are you headed?'

'We were going to Aviemore, but missed a turning,' replied Gareth. He nodded towards Arthur. 'Our map reader only managed to get us to Brigadoon.'

'Brigadoon?' asked Agnes. 'Where's that?'

'It doesn't exist,' interrupted Arthur, 'and it's a long story.'

Hamish laughed. 'Oh no, I know about Brigadoon.' And with a wink at Arthur and a laugh, added, 'I think you and I have been there.'

'Oh no,' said Gareth, 'not another fictional traveller.'

'What are you lot on about?' asked Aileen.

'I'll tell you later,' responded her husband. 'After lunch, we are heading south to Oban.'

'Is there any chance I could join you?' asked Billy. 'I think I have had enough trekking.'

'Amen,' echoed Gareth.

Arthur joined in. 'After being lost for two nights in the Highlands, I too might skip Aviemore and head south.'

'We'll discuss your situation later,' said Conor. 'For now, tell us where you've been.'

They chatted about trekking and campervanning, home and work, until Agnes shouted, 'Lunch.'

* * * * * *

The meal consisted of mince stew followed by apple crumble and custard. Arthur noticed Aileen take her lunch and another plate to one of the campervans and wondered if there was someone else there whom they hadn't met. But he didn't ask.

After lunch, Arthur noticed Conor and Hamish deep in conversation by one of the campervans. Conor shook his head vehemently and looked angry, but Hamish grasped him by the arms and spoke in a way which seemed to appease his brother. A few minutes later, Hamish approached the three travellers.

'Look,' he offered, 'along with our campers, we have a small van which Agnes drove. It held our supplies and other bits and pieces. If you wish, one of you could drive the van and have your equipment in it, and make any further plans when we reach Oban.'

Billy looked pleadingly at Gareth who shrugged, turned to Arthur, and said, 'Why not?'

Arthur nodded in agreement. 'As long as I drive.'

'You're welcome to.' responded Gareth. 'I am exhausted.'

* * * * * *

With the two campervans leading the way, the convoy travelled down the A86, stopping for a comfort break in Fort William.

'We will keep going towards Oban,' said Hamish. 'There is a free-for-one-night campsite about a mile outside the town.'

Three hours after they'd set out, the campervans eventually pulled into the campsite. Conor checked in at the shop/reception and handed Arthur two tickets.

'The tent spot is over to your right; we're straight on a bit. We won't have anything for tea, the kids are exhausted. The shop has plenty on offer food-wise, but you can come to us for breakfast in the morning.'

'No, we have food with us,' replied Arthur. 'And it's Gareth's turn to cook,' he added with a laugh.

They went their separate ways and parked the van. With tents erected, Gareth set up the stove and cooked the remaining sausages and eggs, then the trio sat inside the large tent to eat and discuss their plans for the following day.

'I would like to go on the ferry to Mull and see Tobermory,' said Billy.

'What's in Tobermory?' asked Gareth.

'The painted houses of Balamory,' Billy replied, 'I've only ever seen them on the television.'

'We might as well,' said Arthur, 'and then we can travel down to Glasgow by train from Oban.'

Billy's face lit up as Arthur spoke. 'I've never travelled by train through Scotland before. It will be exciting, and I can get more pictures.'

'Right, see you in the morning,' said Arthur. 'I'm tired. Goodnight.'

* * * * * *

'Come on, you guys,' Arthur called in through the large tent flap. 'Time to get up.'

Half an hour later, he met Gareth and Billy returning from the washhouse.

'Put your stuff in the tent and no cooking this morning,' he said. 'There's a van on the edge of the site, and the guy's cooking smells great. Come on.'

After an English breakfast which they ate outside their tents, the three tidied up and packed their gear in the van then went in search of Hamish and Co., finding them quite easily.

'I will drive the van into Oban for you,' said Arthur, 'and then we are going to Mull. Billy wants to see some painted houses.'

'Well, actually,' said Hamish, 'you can drive the van onto the ferry, because two young people also want to see the painted houses.'

At that, Gavin and Ailsa arrived with their mothers.

Billy went to meet them. 'I believe we are all going to see Balamory? I loved it when I was younger.'

'Oh, great!' shouted Gavin and Ailsa in unison.

* * * * * *

'The ferry from Oban leaves this afternoon for Tobermory,' said Hamish. 'Join us for lunch?'

'No, thanks,' replied Arthur. 'We have enjoyed your hospitality thus far, and with thanks. But I think the guys and I would like to explore Oban. Can we leave our gear in your van?'

'Of course,' replied Hamish. 'But get back here for 1.15pm to get booked in.'

Arthur, Gareth, and Billy waved goodbye and set off to wander through Oban and have lunch.

* * * * * *

Later that day, as the Oban ferry approached Tobermory, Billy pointed towards the town and exclaimed, 'Balamory!'

Arthur and Gareth looked at him in amazement.

'You must remember the children's TV programme? Set here in Tobermory, with Miss Hollie and PC Plum?'

'Oh dear,' groaned Gareth. 'Between Arthur's Brigadoon and now your Balamory, I suddenly feel very old. Don't either of you know of Han Solo, Princess Leia, Luke Skywalker?'

'Yes,' said Arthur and Billy in unison. 'Star Wars!'

'Oh, at last!' Gareth exclaimed. 'At last, we have something in common.' All three burst out laughing.

When the ferry docked, the parties climbed into the vehicles, drove off, and then stopped on the quayside. The children jumped out, shouting, 'Balamory, Balamory!'

Billy turned to his companions. 'There, what did I tell you?'

Hamish explained that Netflix had been running episodes of the children's programme some weeks ago and the children had loved it.

The group left their vehicles and walked along the street of brightly coloured houses. Billy took photographs of the town that he had known as Balamory.

'What do you plan to do?' asked Hamish. 'We are going to visit the religious site on Iona. You're welcome to come.'

'Ok,' Gareth spoke for his two friends, who laughed and agreed.

The ferry from Fionnphort on the Isle of Mull carried the travellers to Iona, but their vehicles had to remain in Fionnphort. A minibus had deposited about a dozen monks, who were also on a visit to the island.

On Iona, the groups split up, and Arthur, Gareth and Billy walked to the Abbey. Although neither of the three had religious inclinations, they couldn't help feeling a sense of awe and spirituality as they explored the building and then the monastery. Leaflets informed them that in 563, Columba had arrived on Iona from Ireland with 12 companions, and founded the monastery. The leaflets explained much more about Iona and the Christians who lived and worked there.

When their time was up, the group caught the ferry back to Mull then, back in their vehicles, boarded the next ferry to Oban. Arthur watched as the habit-clad monks boarded their minibus, but something caused him to frown. Shouts from his friends to hurry up, put the questions from his mind.

On the quay, Arthur, Gareth, and Billy parted company with Hamish, Conor, and their families, thanking them for their generosity and companionship on the trip.

As he returned the van and waited for Hamish to collect the keys, Arthur caught sight of a pale face peering out of his campervan. Too young for Aileen, and too old for Ailsa. But he thought to himself, *None of my business.*

Reunited with their camping gear, Arthur, Gareth, and Billy caught the train to Glasgow.

* * * * * *

The train journey from Oban to Glasgow took just over three hours, during which Arthur and Billy slept, but not Gareth. He felt a stirring within him that suggested he might like to return to Iona. Perhaps he could spend a while at the 'Retreat' he had read about in his leaflet.

CHAPTER 3

The next train journey took the three travellers from Glasgow to Birmingham, where they shook hands and parted company. Arthur offered to return the camping equipment, and picked up his car at the paid-for car park, while Gareth and Billy caught buses to their separate destinations.

At home, as he unpacked his knapsack, Billy discovered the package and the note.

Dear Billy,

I had planned to post this package, but when I discovered you lived in Solihull, I wondered if you would deliver it to my friend. It is a particular medicine that he can only get in Scotland, and when he discovered my plans, asked me to buy him some.

The address is 24 Willard Avenue.

We enjoyed your company. Pass on our regards to Arthur and Gareth.

Your recent friend,
Hamish

Billy recognised the address as being just a few streets from where he lived, and the following afternoon he called round with the parcel.

'Ah, thank you,' said the recipient. 'Hamish phoned and told me you would deliver it.'

Suddenly, sirens sounded, and two police cars appeared. The occupant grabbed the package, pushed Billy to the ground, and slammed the door.

A policeman hauled Billy to his feet. 'What were you doing here?' he asked.

'Delivering a package from a friend in Scotland,' Billy replied, his face white with fear.

'Do you know what the package contained?' the policeman asked.

'Yes,' replied Billy, 'medicine for the man who lived here. It came with a note.'

Billy pulled the note from his pocket and handed it to the officer.

After reading the note, he said, 'You are either a good liar or very naïve.'

Just then, the front door opened and two police officers appeared with the occupant in handcuffs.

'Caught him trying to climb over the next-door garden wall,' one officer stated.

'Do you know who this is, Billy?' Having read the note, the policeman knew Billy's name.

'No,' replied Billy.

'Never mind. Come with us to the station, and you will find out,' he responded. And to Billy's relief, the man did not handcuff him.

* * * * * *

At the police station, in Interview Room 1, Detective Inspector Atkins sat opposite the man from 24 Willard Avenue.

'Mr Andrew Doherty,' he began, 'who is Hamish?'

'No comment,' Doherty replied. He gave the same reply to all the inspector's questions.

'As you wish,' concluded Atkins, eventually. 'I will formally charge you with possession and distribution of Class A drugs. Other charges may follow when we have completed the search of your house.'

He left the interview room and headed for Interview Room 2, where Billy sat nervously waiting.

'Right, Billy,' began the man. 'I am Detective Inspector Ken Atkins. Tell me, did you honestly not know that the package you delivered contained drugs?'

'Ooh,' responded Billy with his head in his hands. 'I honestly thought it had medicine in it.'

'Who is Hamish?' asked the DI.

'A man with a family we met in Scotland,' replied Billy.

'We?' asked DI Atkins. 'Who's we?'

So Billy told the DI the story of the journey to and through Scotland.

'I tell you what,' said Atkins, 'wait here a minute.'

A constable entered the room as DI Atkins left. A few minutes later, he returned with a pad and pen.

'Two things I want you to do,' Atkins said, handing Billy his mobile phone. 'Ring and ask your friends to come into the station to corroborate your story; they may remember something important. Then, put what you've told me in a statement. I'll leave you in the company of Constable Burns.'

The DI left the room, and Billy looked at Constable Burns, who said, 'Phone first, please.'

Billy only had Gareth's number, so he called him and heard Gareth gasp in amazement as he told his story.

'Right,' Gareth responded, 'I'll phone Arthur, and we'll come in.'

Billy, meanwhile, took up the pen and started writing.

The rest of the afternoon involved interviews with Arthur and Gareth, who also gave their statements in writing. Satisfied that Billy had played no part in the drug distribution other than as an innocent courier, the DI allowed the three friends to go home.

In bed that night, Arthur couldn't sleep. He had remembered the van registration number, but not that of the car. Gareth had not been much help at all; his memories seemed to centre only around the island of Iona.

Arthur turned his thoughts to Gillian. He had just finished a lengthy chat with her when Gareth had called about Billy, but he had arranged to meet up with her the following afternoon for coffee at a café near her home.

'So,' he said to himself, 'I'd better sleep.' Eventually, he did.

* * * * * *

At ten o'clock the following morning, Detective Inspector Ken Atkins sat in his office contemplating why drug dealers would visit a religious site when his phone rang.

* * * * * *

Following his shower and shave, Arthur dressed, but as he laced up his shoes, a vision flashed into his mind. He tied his shoelace, then made a phone call.

'Arthur,' said Atkins, when the call was put through, 'believe it or not, you and your trip to Iona were on my mind. What can I do for you?'

'A picture flashed into my mind just now as I was tying my shoelace,' said Arthur.

'Intriguing,' Ken Atkins commented. 'Go on'.

'I had left my friends to visit the toilet and, as I came out, I saw Hamish chatting to a monk. Nothing strange in that, you may think, after all, we were in a monastery. But that's where my shoelace comes in. The monk wore boots – navvy-type boots. The picture left my mind because I heard Gareth call for me to come and see something.'

'Stop there,' Atkins interrupted. 'Just before you rang, the idea of drug dealers in a monastery bothered me. We need to talk.'

'I am on my way to meet my girlfriend, Gillian, in The Coffee House café not far from the police station,' said Arthur.

'I know it,' said the DI. 'I'll be there about 11.'

* * * * * *

Arthur met Gillian outside the café, and greeted her with a kiss and hug. He had just ordered coffee and cake when the door opened and in came Ken Atkins. He walked to their table and, following introductions and refusing coffee, sat down.

With apologies to Gillian, the two men once again went over the visit to Iona. Arthur gave as detailed a description as possible of the monk, but the man had been wearing a hood.

'I do remember something bothering me as I watched the monks boarding their minibus,' Arthur admitted. 'He wasn't with them, because while they wore black habits, he wore brown.'

'You only noticed his boots before,' Ken commented.

'Yes,' responded Arthur, 'isn't memory a funny, and yet wonderful, thing?'

'Right,' said Ken, rising. 'I've already been in touch with our Scottish colleagues. I'll now ask them to make enquiries about a brown-robed, navvy boot-wearing 'monk'.'

He shook hands with Arthur and Gillian and left the café.

CHAPTER 3

A squad car arrived at the Oban ferry terminal, and three constables and an inspector alighted. Enquiries began, and information was gathered.

The lavatory attendant on the Oban quay had observed the 'monk' enter the toilet block that day, and later found a brown robe discarded in one of the cubicles. He also stated that while he'd noticed a monk enter the public toilet, only a workman in overalls had come out.

'I entered the toilet just after he left,' continued the attendant, 'and it was empty. I checked the cubicles, and that's when I found the robe.'

'Did you notice where the workman went?' the police officer asked.

'Yes,' he replied, 'he walked across the square and into the café, but I saw no sign of the monk.' He laughed, 'I remember thinking that he must have got flushed down the toilet.'

'What did you do with the robe?' asked the officer.

* * * * * *

The constable reclaimed the robe from Lost Property and crossed the square to the café where he met up with one of his colleagues and exchanged information. The only item of interest was the story of the monk/workman.

The waitress remembered giving the man in overalls tea and a bun, but could only provide a vague description – he was bald and tanned. She did, however, notice a tattoo of a small dragon on his wrist as he paid at the counter.

The four police officers met up again at their car and, after sharing their information, the inspector decided that they could now disregard the monk and focus on the workman.

Back at their station, a female constable who was known to be a decent artist, produced a drawing of a bald, brown workman, showing him from the shoulders up.

During that afternoon, the constables returned to the square and showed copies of the drawing to passers-by and staff in the nearby shops. At the Bus Depot, they struck gold. A driver remembered a bald passenger in overalls, and with a tan, boarding the bus. But to where, he told the questioning constable, he could not say.

However, he did remember that most of the passengers that afternoon had purchased tickets to Glasgow.

The inspector decided that the information should be passed on to Glasgow.

'I think,' he said to his colleagues, 'that is our job done.'

CHAPTER 4

The email came through to DI Atkins, followed by a phone call from the Glasgow Police HQ. The caller introduced himself as Detective Howard Craig.

'Did you receive an email?' he asked.

'I did,' replied Atkins, 'and it makes interesting reading. The Oban police force did a good job.'

'Indeed,' said Craig, 'and further enquiries have discovered that your brown-robed monk is an engineer on a Glasgow ship, *Cambodia*. His name is Nikel Anderson, and he joined the ship in Portugal.

'However,' continued the Glasgow inspector, 'he did not return to his ship. We believe he caught a train to Birmingham.'

'Oh, that puts him in my jurisdiction now,' replied Atkins. 'Thank you. I'll get wheels put in motion here.'

'But,' said Craig, 'keep me in the loop please.'

'Will do. Goodbye.' Ken Atkins ended the call and immediately brought together his drug squad colleagues, Sergeant Len Billings, and Constables Sharon Williams and Terry Anderson, to bring them up to date and decide on a plan of action.

'It can't be a coincidence that the guy in our cells and this brown-skinned fellow don't know each other,' said Billings.

'Sir,' said Sharon. 'With a name like Nikel, he must have Indian connections.'

'So,' said Ken, 'mother, Indian; father, English?'

'Or Scottish?' Len questioned. 'After all, Anderson is a Scottish surname.'

'And,' continued the DI, 'that could be our Scottish connection to Hamish. Terry, take Anderson's photo to our prisoner,' said Ken, 'and see if he recognises him. Tell him it may help his defence if he co-operates.'

Terry stood outside the cell and talked with Andrew Doherty, who reluctantly rose from his bunk and approached the cell door.

'Do you recognise this man?' Terry asked.

'I want a solicitor,' Doherty replied. 'Get me James Barlow, from Dickson & Dickson. Then I might have something useful to say.'

'But,' insisted Terry, 'do you recognise this man?'

'My solicitor,' said the prisoner, and turned back to his bunk.

* * * * *

The search of Andrew Doherty's house proved fruitful, as he had known it would. A notebook containing names and address proved to be useful.

Next morning, James Barlow arrived at the police station to see his client, and spent some time with Andrew Doherty in Interview Room 1 before DI Atkins and Sergeant Billings entered.

Len Billings switched on the recording machine, and the two officers stated their names and reasons for the interview.

The solicitor James Barlow spoke first. 'My client admits to the charge of drug possession but, for his co-operation, would wish the charge of drug distribution dropped.'

Ken addressed the prisoner. 'Mr Doherty, during the search of your house my officers discovered this.' He held up the notebook. 'Some of the names I am familiar with from previous investigations, and the fact that you also seem to be familiar with those names places you in a difficult position.'

Andrew Doherty wiped his nose. 'I don't know how that book came to be in my house. Perhaps you lot planted it there.'

'Ah,' Ken interrupted, 'and the fact that your fingerprints are all over and inside this book, how would you explain that?'

This time, Doherty wiped not only his nose but his brow. He looked at his solicitor who advised him, under the circumstances, to tell the DI what he had told him.

'Look, Inspector,' he said, 'I am small fry, just a middle-man.' Doherty pointed to the book and continued, 'If you know these guys, you'll know they're big and dangerous. I can give you other names, and times, and dates of transactions, but I want anonymity and witness protection.'

'I will put that to my superiors,' Ken responded.

'But meantime,' said Sergeant Billings, and once again produced the photo of Nikel Anderson, 'do you know this man?'

Doherty stared at it for a while before shaking his head.

'Sorry, gentlemen,' he said, 'not one of mine.'

* * * * * *

Nikel Anderson had indeed travelled to England, but not to Birmingham. That's where the Scottish police had made a mistake. He had caught a train to Liverpool, where he signed on a freighter going to the Azores.

And with no further leads, the drug squad was forced to drop him from their enquiries.

EPILOGUE

Andrew Doherty received his witness protection. Using the names in Doherty's book, police swooped on various locations and made many arrests. The evidence presented by Doherty from behind a screen, and from other sources, resulted in long-term jail sentences for a number of notorious drug dealers.

* * * * * *

With the arrival of Spring, Gillian's mum had deteriorated to such an extent that she and Bet decided a nursing home would be the best place for her. Gillian now worked for another firm, but her romance with Arthur had blossomed.

Gareth returned to Iona, became a 'born again believer' and joined the community there.

Billy continued his university studies, planning to take a degree in engineering. He could not believe that his very secular-minded friend Gareth had become a Christian.

They did, however, keep in contact.

* * * * * *

That same Spring, Arthur received a letter, postmarked Aberdeen.

He opened it and read:

My dear Arthur, greetings.

How I got your address is neither here nor there. Let's just say we both have contacts in Aberdeen.

I feel I owe you an explanation. My daughter Carol told me that you might have seen her looking out of my campervan window in Oban. Because of her serious illness, she fell into a coma on our way to… well, never mind. She only mentioned this to me when she came out of the hospital. I'm afraid she died yesterday.

I wondered if you'd seen me talking to the monk in Iona; I saw his picture just recently in an old copy of a Glasgow newspaper. His name is Nikel, and his mother is my sister. He chose the meeting place and his monk robe disguise.

Anyway, my Carol needed a particular medicine which he could get, but in another country. He had a contact in Birmingham who could get this medicine in… well, let's say again, that other country where Nikel could pick it up. The deal was other drugs that Nikel could lay his hands on for my medicine.

I'm not in Aberdeen now, of course. We as a family are wanderers.

Regards to your friends.
Hamish.

There was no mention of using Billy, but perhaps Hamish thought Arthur would not have known about this.

He decided to burn the letter on the barbeque which was already prepared for today's visitors – Gareth and Billy, amongst others – to announce his engagement to Gillian.

The Daring Young Man

CHAPTER 1

I can only remember one phrase line in that song, 'the daring young man on the flying trapeze'.

Born in and into the circus, I loved to watch the acts, especially the trapeze artists. My name is Ben, and I watched on the day they carried my father's lifeless body from the circus ring. I didn't cry; my mother didn't cry. Indeed, I don't think one of the circus family cried.

* * * * * *

My father arrived at the circus in 1984 as a lad of 16. He had run away from a care home, and hoped to fulfil his heart's desire – to join a circus.

Carl Ferguson, the circus owner and ringmaster, looked him up and down.

'What's your name, and where have you come from?' he asked my dad.

'Andy Erskine,' lied my dad, using the name of the care home's vile attendant who was an abuser and the reason for my dad's escape.

It turned out that Carl needed someone to clean the elephant house – a messy job, and one from which his previous employee had absconded without notice, after receiving his pay. And so, my dad began working with the circus.

Unfortunately, he had an aggressive attitude which made him few friends. Except for Jenny, the owner's 12-year-old daughter, who loved elephants and often came to watch Andy at work. She told him that one day she hoped to be an elephant trainer; he said that one day he would be a trapeze artist. They laughed and joked together about their plans.

Carl, however, did not approve of the friendship. Jenny had attended several primary schools as the circus moved around, but now Carl felt she needed further and regular education, so he hired a tutor named Wendy. Jenny proved to be a bright girl and studied well, gaining a degree through Open University.

Meanwhile, Andy moved from dung cleaning to elephant training.

Jenny loved watching Christine, the acrobat who rode and performed somersaults on the backs of the giant elephants. 'Someday,' she said to herself, 'someday.'

* * * * * *

One evening, as Carl walked past the entrance to the big top, he heard a sound from the ring. Walking in, he stared as Andy swung from trapeze to trapeze with perfect timing. He waited until Andy had landed on the platform before calling, 'What do you think you're doing? Come down at once.'

Andy descended and walked towards Carl. 'What did you think of that?' he asked cheekily.

'I should fire you on the spot,' replied Carl. 'I have no insurance to cover amateurs using my equipment, and doing so without a safety net.'

But his face relaxed into the semblance of a smile. 'Where did you learn to fly like that?'

'On the bars in the park playground,' replied Andy. 'My mates used to call me the monkey. And this is not the first time I've practised in the evenings before performances.'

'Go on,' scolded Carl. 'Get to bed. And get those elephants ready for tomorrow afternoon.'

Andy left the ring with a smirk on his face. He had put one over on his boss and got away with it.

* * * * * *

During holidays from her studies, Jenny would learn from Christine as she rode and performed her somersaults on the backs of the bigger elephants. Carl looked on at the practices with a sense of pride.

Jenny's mother, his late wife, had performed like that until cancer had taken her from them.

The following day, the afternoon programme, especially the clowns and the magician, went down well with the children. The evening one had more adult themes, including advanced trapeze acts, the lion tamer, and the elephant performances.

During practice, Greg, one the 'Trapeziairs', hurt his wrist, so the afternoon performance only involved Hans the German catcher and Heide, his niece. But between performances, Carl chatted with Hans regarding trying out with Andy.

At first, Andy did his usual loops and catches. Then Hans tried him with a somersault and hand grab. Andy turned out to be a natural, so it was decided that he would take Greg's place that evening. The group practised several moves using Heidi and Andy, and all worked well.

The act continued until Greg's wrist recovered and then, unlike him, Andy graciously stepped down and went back to his elephants.

But, unknown to Carl, his daughter and Andy had become a secret item, until Andy asked Jenny to marry him. They both approached Carl, who fumed at the prospect, but Jenny insisted.

'Dad,' she argued, 'I'm 19 now. I've obeyed you and completed my studying and earned a degree. I want to marry Andy. I love him and have done for some time.'

'Carl,' Andy said, 'I love your daughter and will look after her. We will stay with the circus, and perhaps I could become your assistant.'

Jenny approached her dad and hugged him. 'Please, Dad, give us your blessing.'

'Well,' he told Andy, 'you wouldn't have been my choice, kid. But if you promise to look after my daughter and love her, I may give you my blessing.'

Jenny ran to Andy and hugged him. 'Now, we can set a date.'

Dislike for Andy over the years had grown amongst the other circus staff, and their faces showed both surprise and concern when the news spread.

Carlos and Jeremy, the circus clowns, were especially displeased. They had known and played with Jenny since her childhood, but if Carl had agreed, they knew they would have to learn to accept it.

* * * * * *

Following the wedding, Jenny took over the acrobatic display, following Christine's instructions to the letter.

Andy, due to Jenny's persuasion, became Carl's assistant but kept up his trapeze practice. And with Greg's permission, he took an occasional turn on the trapeze.

The years passed and in 1999, Jenny gave up her act. Seven months later, she gave birth to – me.

CHAPTER 2

When I turned two, Carl died in his bed. The circus doctor, Doctor Michael McClean, who knew that Carl had a weak heart, wrote 'heart failure' on the death certificate. The circus remained in the one location until after the burial.

Carl's will left the circus to his daughter Jenny. Any cash he had was to be divided between the circus funds and me. The cash proved to be small in quantity, and the circus was in debt. However, although my mother owned the circus, it was my dad who controlled the running of it.

He always looked on the internet at YouTube circus acts and made copious copies of the routines. Then the various troupes had to watch evening video shows which Andy commanded they would copy. Practice followed practice before the circus opened again to the public.

Many of the new acts proved to be more advanced and dangerous than before, but the public loved them. The crowds grew in number, and the money came rolling in. I now had a nursemaid while Mum resumed her career.

By the time I reached the age of 10, the circus had changed acts a few times but its success proved phenomenal.

No more babies joined our family, but Andy's popularity dwindled. He started drinking and became abusive to Mum and me. One drunken evening, my dad told me his real name – Billy Cairns. But of his family, he would say nothing. 'After all, they put me into care,' he said.

Then came the fateful evening. After ranting and raving at the circus crew, and especially the trapeze team, Andy decided he would show them what he wanted them to do. Even after a few drinks, his skill on the trapeze held the onlookers in admiration.

On his final flight, however, his landing on the platform faltered, and he staggered and fell off the edge. His fall took him past the end of the safety net, and he crashed to the side of the ring. By the shape of his crumpled body, the onlookers knew the outcome.

And Billy Cairns, alias Andy Erskine, would fly no more.

* * * * * *

To my dismay, Mum sold the circus, and she and I settled down in Sheffield. I joined a local theatre and became quite famous as an actor. You'll not have heard of me, because all the names used in this story are fictitious. Although my mum has passed away, I am still around — but who can guess my name?

The Amazing Adventures
of Murphy
the Magnificent
and Friends

INTRODUCTION

Marvo felt very sad. He was an excellent magician and had made many people gasp with wonder at his tricks. But now he felt sad, because many of his magician friends were using their powers to help people who were selfish and greedy.

He felt not just sad but old and tired. He thought to himself, *I think I'll retire and use my magic for doing good in the world.*

Marvo lived in a mansion with many rooms, one of which he made into a laboratory of magic. There, he invented thousands of coloured sweets that had special powers. Power to make you mighty, to make you grow, to fly, to change your appearance. Whoever ate them would do wonders, but only good deeds, and help to make the world a better place in which to live.

Life, however, proved short for Marvo. He tapped himself with his wand and disappeared, re-appearing in the land for retired wizards.

CHAPTER 1

The Adventures Begin:

On a hillside, not far from a large water storage dam, stood the Murphy farm. Farmer and Mrs Murphy had lived and worked there for many years. Their children had all grown up and gone away to work in the big city. None of the Murphy family children wanted to stay and work on the farm. Farmer and Mrs Murphy were not alone, however. They had Spark, the collie dog, and Ginger, their rather lazy cat. And behind the scullery door, through a hole in the wall, was the home of the mouse family. Many times, the oldest mouse in the family would venture out looking for food, and Ginger would try to catch him. But not once did Ginger even come near to capturing the all-too-quick Master Mouse.

One day Farmer Murphy came into the house looking very worried.

'My dear wife, I'm afraid our home and farm are in danger.'

'Why, what is wrong?' asked Mrs Murphy.

Farmer Murphy told her that the wall of the dam had cracked, and heavy rain had caused the streams feeding the dam to burst their banks.

Then he said, 'It won't be long before the dam bursts and our farm and the village below will be right in the path of the flood.' With a frown, he continued, 'Everyone in the village is moving to higher ground, and so must we.'

* * * * *

When Master Mouse came out from behind the scullery door, all was quiet. No Ginger! No Spark! And no sign of Farmer and Mrs Murphy or the farmyard animals.

'Yes!' shouted Master Mouse, as he scampered through the farmhouse gathering all kinds of bits of food: bread, a wee bit of cheese, the end of a sausage lying beside the bin.

'This is amazing!' he said to his family.

So, for a whole week, and without disturbance, the mouse family feasted on their fantastic store of food. That is, until the day the dam wall burst. Water came cascading down the hillside, carrying branches and sods and all kinds of everything in its path. The mouse family had just finished their evening meal when suddenly, the scullery door burst open, and a torrent of water swept through and into the kitchen and the living room. The flow then crashed through the front door and windows, taking with it the remaining bits and pieces of furniture – and the mouse family.

* * * * *

As the water swept Master Mouse away, he looked around but couldn't see any of his family. Just then, a piece of kitchen chair went by, and he grabbed it and climbed on, using it as a boat. Again, he looked all around, but there was no sign of his family. Master Mouse clung on to the piece of a chair until he was so tired he could hold on no longer, and slipped once again into the water. The flow now, however, was not so steady, and with what little strength he had left, he swam towards an overhanging branch. Thankfully, he reached it and clambered up out of the water.

Exhausted, Master Mouse lay gasping on what was now the bank of the river, and wet though he was, he fell asleep. When he awoke, the sun was shining, and the water was no longer flowing. As he looked around, he could see steps and, at the top, what looked like a castle. Now dried out, Master Mouse felt hungry and decided to climb the steps in search of food. It took a long time to reach the top, but when he did he saw, to his delight, a gap under the door of the castle through which he could squeeze.

Once inside, he found another door which was very slightly open, and through the opening, he could see flickering light. Cautiously, Master Mouse crept towards the door and peeped into a large room. The flickering light came from a fire, and Master Mouse decided to warm himself before looking for food. To his astonishment, beside the fire there was a plate with bread, milk, and the most significant piece of cheese he had ever seen in his whole life! It wasn't too long before, warmed and well-fed, he lay down beside the fire and fell fast asleep.

* * * * * *

Master Mouse could not be sure if what happened next was real or only a dream, but in the room there appeared a shimmering figure.

The figure spoke. 'Hello, little friend, my name is Marvo and I am a magician. I live in a land far away. However, I saw what happened to you. Now that you are here, I want to tell you about your future. But first, what is your name?'

As though in a dream, Master Mouse opened his mouth to speak, when he realised that he didn't have a name. Then the name Murphy came into his mind, so he answered, 'Murphy'.

The shimmering figure, not the person of Marvo, but a magical image spoke.

'Well then, young Murphy, follow me.'

Still not sure if he was awake or dreaming, Master Mouse, now known as Murphy, followed Marvo out of the room and up the stairs. Murphy found himself in the most fantastic place. All around the walls, there were glass jars full of brightly coloured sweets. Marvo then told Murphy about them and their special powers and that he, Murphy, would now possess these special powers each time he ate a sweet. But he could only use the skills to do good deeds.

Suddenly Murphy seemed to wake up, and he was in the room with the coloured sweets. He looked around, but the image of Marvo had disappeared. Somehow, though, Murphy knew exactly what to do, where to go, and what to take with him. As he stood gazing at the jars, something told him to close his eyes tightly. He did, and when he opened his eyes, he had changed.

Murphy found himself inside a tent, dressed in a jacket and trousers, and with a little cap on his head. In the jacket pocket, he found lots of coloured sweets.

His adventure as Murphy the Magnificent had begun.

CHAPTER 2

Murphy and the School Robber:

Murphy opened the door of his tent. It had been a busy week, what with fighting a crocodile to rescuing a fisherman, yes — a crocodile. How it got into the river, nobody knew, but now Murphy had sent it back to where it belonged. Then there was the foolish boy who stood up in the Ferris wheel and fell out of the cab; another one to rescue before he hit the ground. They were just two of the many ways that Murphy the Magnificent had used his powers to help others. But that is why he had the sweets with their magic powers. Murphy had returned to the mansion many times since that first meeting with the image of Marvo; on each visit, he filled his bag and pockets with more special sweets.

Murphy now put his memories aside and had almost fallen asleep when he heard his name called. Opening his eyes, he saw Conor and his sister Holly coming up the hill towards him. Murphy loved it when they came to visit, although their visits always seemed to end with an adventure.

'Hello, Murphy!' shouted Conor.

'Hello, Murphy!' echoed Holly.

'Why are you two not at school?' asked Murphy.

'Well,' said Holly, 'that's what we've come to see you about.'

'Yes,' Conor interrupted. 'We went to school this morning, but when we got there our teachers were scratching their heads in wonder.'

'You see.' continued Holly,' the school had disappeared!'

'You'd better come and see for yourself,' said Conor.

* * * * * *

Off went Murphy, Conor, and Holly to find out why and how the school had disappeared. When they arrived, they found everyone looking very bewildered — they couldn't understand how a whole building could just vanish.

Murphy wondered if it had. So he put his hand in his pocket and took out a yellow sweet. He knew that it would help him to see things other people couldn't see, and sure enough, Murphy noticed that the school hadn't vanished. An invisible curtain stretched right around the school.

To everyone but Murphy, the school had gone. Then he noticed something else, or someone else, behind the invisible curtain. A person that Murphy had come up against before. It was Robbie Robbin, and that is what this person did – rob people and places. The last time Murphy had tangled with him was when Robbie had somehow put the staff of the local bank to sleep and been about to take all the money until Murphy had stopped him. Now he would have to stop him again.

Taking Holly and Conor by their hands, he walked them away from the crowd. 'Now, Holly and Conor,' Murphy said, 'this is what is happening.' And he told them all about Robbie the robber.

'This time, however,' Murphy continued, 'he has his gang with him, so I will need your help'.

* * * * * *

Murphy put his hand in his pocket and took out a purple sweet for Holly and a green one with black spots for Conor. Immediately, changes took place; Holly became a large, round purple ball, and Conor was a Red Indian warrior.

'Come on,' called Murphy, 'follow me.' As he ran, Murphy put his hand in his pocket and took out and ate a red sweet. 'Red for strength!' he shouted, as the three heroes rolled, leapt, and ran to where Robbie and his gang were loading their stolen school treasures into a white van.

The gang didn't know what hit them as a big purple ball rolled over two of them, flattening them into the ground. A whooping Indian warrior then shot rubber-tipped arrows at two more, knocking them down with the arrows stuck to their heads.

Robbie Robbin, the robber, dropped what he was carrying and tried to run, but Murphy grabbed him by his trouser belt, and although his legs were moving he couldn't run anywhere.

Murphy gave him a slight tap on the head, which made him see stars in front of his eyes. Now Robbie's powers had gone, and the invisible curtain became visible.

The crowd couldn't believe their eyes; the school had suddenly re-appeared.

Meanwhile, the purple ball went back to being Holly, and Conor once again became Conor. The police arrived and arrested Robbie and his gang. 'Congratulations,' said the chief of police to Holly and Conor. 'I don't know how you did it, but you captured a dangerous gang and saved the school's treasures and dinner money.'

The Chief then put his hand in his pocket and brought out two medals.

'These are police bravery awards,' he said, 'well done, the two heroes!'

He then pinned one on Holly and the other on Conor. The watching crowd clapped and cheered.

The Chief then turned to Murphy.

'Once again,' he said, 'a big thank you to you. You are magnificent.'

* * * * * *

With everything now back to normal, the children began filing into school.

Murphy turned to Holly and Conor and said, 'What an adventure.' Then sadly, he said,' I won't be seeing you for a while. I have to leave, because my help is needed in another place.'

Seeing their sad faces, he told them, 'Cheer up! We will meet up again someday, and hopefully enjoy another adventure. Goodbye!' And with that, Murphy waved and started up the hill to his tent.

Once inside, he closed his eyes very tightly. Now, there are different reasons why people close their eyes. Some do it to go to sleep; others to shut out something they don't want to see. But when Murphy closed his eyes tightly, it was because he knew he was going on another mission to another place to help another person.

CHAPTER 3

Murphy and The Marsh Monster:

Murphy opened the door of his tent. It was another lovely day, but where was he? There was no green grass and no sign of life.

Murphy began walking down the hill from his tent. The ground was soft, and the earth black. At the bottom of the mountain, the land became marshy, and he was glad he was a mouse; anyone dense would surely sink here.

'Don't go any further,' a voice shouted. 'The thing will get you.'

Looking up, Murphy saw a boy in the branches of a tree.

'Come over here quickly,' the boy shouted.

Murphy didn't know what was going on, or who 'the thing' might be. But, curious, he made his way towards the tree. He could feel the ground begin to shake, so quickly climbed up beside the boy.

Suddenly, out of the marshy ground, there emerged a great big head with two glowing red eyes which began looking around.

'He heard you,' said the boy. 'Now follow me.'

With that, he climbed down inside the tree. Murphy quickly followed him, and soon he found himself in a long tunnel. Although it had little light, he could just make out the boy up ahead so Murphy moved a little faster to keep up with him. They moved upwards through the tunnel until the boy turned to the right and entered a large cave, then stopped.

'Now,' he said, entirely out of breath, 'welcome to safety.'

'Safety from what?' asked Murphy.

'Didn't you see it?' shouted the boy. 'The Marsh Monster!'

'Oh! Is that what it was?' replied Murphy.

'Were you not frightened?' the boy asked.

'Not really,' said Murphy. 'I've seen more frightening things than that.'

'What!' exclaimed the boy. 'Oh, by the way, who are you? I've never seen a mouse as tall as you and wearing clothes.'

'Never mind me,' said Murphy, 'what are you doing here?'

'My name is Jack, 'the boy said, 'and back in our town, my brother Ethan and I heard stories of a marsh and a monster. We listened to the stories from our grandparents, who had heard them from their parents. Ethan and I decided to go and look for it. Just as we thought of doing so, we suddenly found ourselves in this strange place.'

Ah, Murphy thought to himself, *sounds like Marvo's doing.*

'And where is your brother?' asked Murphy.

Just then, another boy came out from the back of the cave, carrying two books. He stared wide-eyed at Murphy; he'd never seen a mouse who looked like this one.

Jack introduced him. 'This is my brother Ethan, and this is a very peculiar mouse whose name I don't know.'

'Hello, Ethan,' said Murphy, 'my name is Murphy, and I have come to help the people of this place.'

'Pleased to meet you,' Ethan responded. 'Who sent you, and how did you know they needed help?'

Murphy told them who he was and how he came to be there.

Ethan said, 'Well, if you are going to help, maybe you should try and read this old book.'

Ethan again explained how they had mysteriously found themselves in the caves. They'd had no idea where to look for this so-called monster, but as they'd approached the marsh, suddenly they the beast had risen from the ground.

Jack took up the story. 'We saw and climbed the only tree around. It's a good job we were wearing our wellies, because the land was so soft and so wet.'

He went on, 'The monster started towards us, but stopped before it came near the tree. Then it just growled and turned and went back into the marsh. Ethan went back to the cave, but I stayed a while at the top of the tree. That is when I saw you walking towards the marsh. The rest you know.'

Ethan had found the book he was carrying inside the trunk of the tree which he and Jack had climbed when they first saw the monster. The book, however, was written in an old type of English which the boys couldn't fully understand.

'From what we could make out, the monster made the townspeople supply it with food,' Jack continued, 'but it didn't eat meat, so harmed no people or animals. That was as far as we could get; we couldn't make out the rest.'

'It's funny, though,' Ethan said thoughtfully. 'Although the monster ate all the other vegetation, it never comes near this tree.'

'Can I see the book?' asked Murphy.

'Of course,' said Ethan, and he gave the book to Murphy. Sure enough, although Murphy could read some of the book, like Jack and Ethan, he couldn't read any further. He turned to the back of the book and noticed some strange symbols.

'Yes, we noticed them, too,' said Jack, 'but hadn't a clue what they were.'

'I'll think about these later,' said Murphy, 'but right now I need to read this book.'

Murphy put his hand in his pocket and took out a white sweet. He knew when he ate it he would gain wisdom and knowledge. Immediately, Murphy began to read all that the book contained. He learned about the history of the Marsh Monster, what it was, where it came from, and why it was here now! While Murphy was reading, Ethan and Jack looked on in astonishment but said nothing.

When he had finished reading, Murphy turned to Jack and Ethan and said, 'Boys, let me tell you a story.'

'Yes, but first,' said Jack, 'will you tell us about the sweet?'

'Ah!' responded Murphy. 'You see, these are special sweets of different colours, given to me by a magician named Marvo. They give me, and whoever eats them, special powers, but only to do good deeds.'

'Can we have one?' asked Ethan and Jack in unison.

'Perhaps later, if needed,' replied Murphy. 'But first, the Marsh Monster.'

* * * * * *

Pulling up some nearby chairs, the three sat down and Murphy began. 'Now, once upon a time the land you see all around was meadow and farmland. At that time, the land belonged to a kind baron who looked after his tenants very well. One day, the baron had a visit from a neighbouring landowner who wanted to buy some of his lands. It was land where some of the baron's best tenants lived, so he refused to sell.

'The landowner was furious and told the baron he would be sorry. The baron then had another visitor – a strange-looking man. The baron didn't know, but the landowner had employed this wizard to do evil. He asked the baron to show him the land that the landowner wanted.

'The baron asked him, "Why?"

'"Oh, just curious," said the wizard.

'But, when they came to the place, the wizard produced a wand and waved it over the ground. Suddenly, the farmland and the meadows became the marsh that you see now. The furious baron watched as his land and his tenants disappeared into the marshy ground. The wizard then turned his wand on the baron who, believe it or not, became the tree where I first saw you, Jack.'

'Oh, I see' said Jack. 'But why does the Marsh Monster not eat this tree?'

'Ah!' replied Murphy, 'why don't we ask the Marsh Monster?'

Murphy already knew the answer. For some reason, the wizard had put a protection on the baron but, at present, Murphy couldn't see why.

'How do we do that?' asked Ethan.

'We go into the marsh,' replied Murphy. But he knew they were not going in to have a conversation with the monster, but to lure it out.

'And how do we do that without drowning?' asked Jack.

Murphy put his hand in his pocket and took out three blue sweets. He gave one each to Ethan and Jack, and took one himself.

'Eat up,' said Murphy.

Within minutes, all three began to take on a frog-like appearance. Ethan and Jack looked at each other in astonishment, and all they could say was 'Wow!'

'Now,' said Murphy, 'let's enter the marsh.'

Down the three frog-like creatures went into the swamp.

The magic sweets helped them to breathe and to see in the murky depths. They swam through the marshy water until suddenly in front of them appeared the Marsh Monster, its two great eyes glowing.

'Now,' signalled Murphy, 'back.'

Jack, Ethan, and Murphy swam with all their might, closely followed by the monster. As soon as they reached the tree, the frog creatures magically changed back into their own bodies, and up they climbed. The Marsh Monster rose out of the marsh and came with a low, growling sound towards the tree.

'I think it is getting bolder, but I want to keep him close by,' said Murphy.

So, he put his hand in his pocket and pulled out two sweets. One, a yellow sweet, he gave to Ethan, who shouted as he ate it, 'I want to be a Viking warrior!' In a flash, there stood Ethan looking like a Thor god, complete with hammer.

'Wow!' exclaimed Jack. As he ate his sweet, he shouted, 'Centurion!' And he became a Roman soldier, with full armour and a sword and shield.

'Now,' said Murphy, 'keep the monster occupied while I get some more help.' With that, he closed his eyes tightly and promptly disappeared.

Jack the Centurion and Thor Ethan didn't notice he had gone; they were too busy in combat with the Marsh Monster. As they circled the monster, Ethan struck with his hammer and Jack with his sword and, although their blows landed, the beast didn't flinch. It did, however, draw away growling and with its eyes flashing. The flashes came towards Jack and Ethan, but Jack warded them off with his shield.

Murphy, meanwhile, opened his eyes and found himself outside Holly and Conor's house. He called their names and out they came.

As they ran to meet him, they called out,' Hello, Murphy, great to see you.'

'Do you need us?' Conor asked.

'Indeed, I do,' replied Murphy, 'and so do Ethan and Jack. But first, go and put on your wellies.'

On their return, Murphy took hold of Conor's and Holly's hands. As he did so, he said, 'Now, close your eyes tightly and don't open them until I tell you, or our magic won't work.' As they closed their eyes tightly, Holly and Conor knew they were off on another adventure.

* * * * * *

When Murphy was sure that they had arrived at their destination, he told Conor and Holly to open their eyes. They were shocked to see the monster, then they watched in amazement as Thor Ethan and Jack the Centurion slowly circled the beast.

'Don't leave this tree till I return,' said Murphy. 'I'll be back soon.'

Murphy left them and went to the cave, where he took the book in his hands. He then put his hand in his pocket and took out a white sweet. Murphy closed his eyes, but this time not to travel, but to think using the wisdom and knowledge that the white sweet gave him.

He opened the book and began to think, 'weed, weed, weeds', trying to conjure a picture of where he might find the plant that the monster hated. With the book in his hands, he was able to see in his mind the evil wizard of the past waving his wand and making the weed disappear.

Concentrating very hard, Murphy suddenly saw another picture – a cave, and not too far away. Inside the cave, and growing everywhere, he could see the particular weed.

Returning to the tree, Murphy said to Holly and Conor, 'Right, come with me.' Taking hold of their hands, he whisked them to the cave and the weed.

Holly asked, 'What's happening? And what was that monster? And who were the people fighting it?'

'Too many questions,' replied Murphy. 'For now, just trust me. We need to gather as much of this weed as we can carry.'

Once again, Murphy put his hand in his pocket and pulled out three sweets, which were kind of indigo in colour. At first, Holly thought they were purple.

'Oh,' she exclaimed, 'I'm going to be a purple ball.'

'No you're not,' laughed Conor, 'that's not a purple sweet, it's indigo. I know my rainbow colours! Let's see what it can do!'

With that, he, Holly, and Murphy (smiling, because he knew what would happen) swallowed their sweets. Immediately, their hands began to grow – or, in Murphy's case, paws. Using their large hands, the three adventurers began scooping up bunches of weed.

'Now', said Murphy, 'touch hands.'

As they did so, they were once again flying back to the marsh. When they arrived, they could see that Thor Ethan and Jack the Centurion were still bravely battling the monster, but getting tired.

Murphy said, 'Quickly, throw your weed at the monster.'

As they did so, the monster immediately retreated into the marsh. When this happened, Ethan and Jack became themselves. They collapsed, breathless, on the ground and were surprised to see Holly and Conor. Like Murphy, they now had normal-sized hands (and paws).

Murphy explained the weed to Jack and Ethan then told them to spread it around the edges of the marsh. Once that was done, they all went back to the cave, where Murphy again picked up the book.

* * * * * *

He turned to the part with the symbols. 'I was thinking,' he said. 'If the wizard had protected the baron by turning him into a tree – albeit a special tree – I wonder if he has left us a clue about something else protective.'

He looked thoughtful. 'You see,' Murphy went on, 'I think the wizard had to do the bidding of that evil landlord but secretly hated doing it, and maybe these symbols are a coded message.'

'But how do we break the code?' asked Jack.

'Oh, don't tell me,' said Conor, 'another of your wonderful sweets.'

'Yes, but I think we will all need to put our heads together to solve this puzzle,' Murphy responded.

He put his hand in his pocket and drew out five white sweets.

'Now, after we have taken our sweets, we must all close our eyes and think, think, think!'

* * * * * *

After what seemed a long, long time of thinking, suddenly a picture formed in each of their minds. And even though none of them had ever met him, they all knew it was the wizard from the book.

They all had the same vision in their minds: The wizard stood beside a blackboard. In his hand, he held a piece of chalk. As soon as he put the chalk to the board, it began to write, all by itself. And this is what they watched it write.

'Good evening, children, I'm glad you have managed to break my code with your thoughts. Observe, because I am now going to show you how to get all your good land back from the marsh. Now that the years have passed and the wicked landlord is no more, I can show you what you must do.

'Go out to the marshy land and repeat these words over the marsh. You must all say them together. The coded words are:

The years have passed, the landlord's gone.
The marshy land's been here too long.
So, marsh and monster on your way,
you won't be back another day.
The farming land now re-appear,
There will be crops again next year.

Suddenly, the pictures disappeared from the minds of Ethan, Jack, Conor, Holly, and Murphy. Immediately, the five bold friends went out to the marsh and, in unison, spoke the words the chalk had written.

As soon as they finished speaking, amazing things began to happen. The marsh slowly disappeared, and somewhere, very faintly, they heard the monster's final growl. The ground all around them began to turn a beautiful green, and trees and bushes shot up from the earth. Townsfolk, looking very bewildered, suddenly appeared along with their possessions, and finally so did their lost town. Buildings sprang up all over the place. The people could now live back where they belonged.

There were four 'Wow's' – one from Holly, then Conor, followed closely by one each from Jack and Ethan. Murphy only smiled a knowing smile.

The people all rushed cheering into their new town, finding homes in which to live; the shopkeepers had shops to open; the clergyman now had a church for prayer; the children found a new school. Everyone had something special to enjoy.

* * * * * *

The townsfolk had no idea how this incredible happening had occurred, but they all came, rejoicing, out of the town to thank their wonderful hero friends. But when they arrived, they noticed that the tree had vanished, and the cave – and of course, that meant the book had gone, too. So many strange things had happened that day that no-one seemed surprised.

Murphy turned to his companions and said, 'Time to go home.' So, once again, eyes were tightly shut and quick as a flash, Holly, Conor, Jack, and Ethan found themselves back in their familiar streets. But, of Murphy, there was no sign. They knew, however, that someday, they would all share another adventure.

Mama Goose and the Skinny Man

CHAPTER 1

Skinny Man Meets Mama Goose:

Mama Goose was the only goose on the farm. There were ducks and hens and all kinds of farm animals, but she couldn't gaggle with them. How she longed for someone to chat to, have a cup of goose tea with, but there was no-one. That is until the day Skinny Man appeared.

He came looking for work, but Mr Farmer smiled and said, 'You don't look strong enough for farm work.'

Taking pity on him, Mr Farmer went on, 'Tell you what, I do need someone to look after my poultry and animals, so would you like to do that?'

'Oh yes!' said Skinny Man, and off he went to meet up with his charges.

The first one he met was a very sad looking Mama Goose. She looked up, expecting to hear the sort of noises humans make when talking to animals, but to her surprise, when he spoke she knew what he was saying.

'Now then, Mrs Goose,' he said, 'why are you looking so sad?'

'Sad! Who's sad?' replied Mama Goose. 'I have now found someone I can talk with.'

'Well, perhaps you could show me around,' said Skinny Man. 'Maybe you would introduce me to all the animals.'

'Delighted!' said Mama Goose, and proudly began the introductions.

Although Mama Goose couldn't understand how it was that this human could speak to animals and birds, she was delighted. First, they visited the hens, then the ducks. The turkey was next, although there was only one of his kind left — next, the pigs and the cows.

'And finally,' said Mama Goose, 'the latest addition, Nettie our foal donkey. Her mum isn't well at present, but you can meet her later.'

So, with that Mama Goose waddled off, with Skinny Man following, around the barn and through the gate to the field.

'There,' said Mama Goose. 'Meet Nettie!'

'Where?' asked Skinny Man.

'Why, there,' said Mama Goose. But when she looked, she couldn't believe her eyes. Nettie had gone. The big farm horse, whose name was Bobby, trotted over.

'Have you seen Nettie?' asked Mama Goose.

'Yes,' replied Bobby, 'Two men came this morning and led her away. I thought they were taking her to see her mum.'

'Oh dear! Oh dear!' cried Mama Goose, 'What shall we do? What are we going to say to Mrs Donkey? Who would have taken her?'

'Let's calm down and think about this,' said Skinny Man. 'It's not who would have taken her but where?'

'There's a market in the village today,' said Bobby. 'I'll bet you that's where they have taken her.'

'I have to tell Mr Farmer,' said Skinny Man.

'You can't' said Bobby. 'I saw Mr and Mrs Farmer driving off just before you came into the field.'

'Oh dear,' said Mama Goose, flapping her wings. 'If I were younger, I would fly to that market and do something, but I don't know what.'

'Tell you what,' said Bobby. 'With Mr Farmer away, he won't be needing me today, so why don't you two climb on my back and I will take you to the market.'

'Good plan!' exclaimed Skinny Man. 'Let's go!'

And with that, Skinny Man climbed up on to Bobby's back, and Mama Goose flew up to join him. Soon they were galloping through the country roads towards the village market.

They arrived to find the village square crowded, so Bobby said, 'I will wait here. You two go on by yourselves.'

With difficulty, Mama Goose and Skinny Man pushed their way through the crowd, although people made way for them thinking that the man was taking the goose to sell at the market.

As they arrived at the rail surrounding the sales ring, Mama Goose pointed excitedly with her wing.

'Look, over by the shed, that's Nettie!' she exclaimed.

'Shush,' said Skinny Man. 'She's not coming up for sale just yet, so keep your eyes on things while I go and make a phone call.'

Off went Skinny Man, and Mama Goose watched carefully at the goings-on in the sales ring.

A cow was sold, then a pony, and as Mama Goose watched, she saw Nettie being led out into the ring.

'Oh! Where are you, Skinny Man?' Mama Goose muttered to herself. 'Nettie, oh Nettie, what can I do?'

There was still no sign of him, so Mama Goose flew up on to the railing and began to hiss loudly. Everyone around began to move away, because they knew the sound of an angry goose. The salesman took Nettie back into the shed, and the chargehands rushed to capture the goose before someone was hurt. But Mama Goose wasn't planning to hurt anyone; she was just glad her ruse had worked as she saw the man returning.

Skinny Man assured the chargehands that he was in control and lifted a now quiet Mama Goose down. He ducked under the rail, went up to the salesman, and whispered something into his ear. He then carried Mama Goose back and under the railing.

The salesman went to the shed and led Nettie out once more into the ring. Mama Goose began to get very agitated but once again, Skinny Man said, 'Shush, just listen.'

'Ladies and gentlemen,' called out the salesman, 'I have learned that this is a foal stolen from a nearby farm, and it is therefore not for sale.'

Skinny Man, who watched the crowd, saw two guilty-looking men slinking away. He signalled to the policemen at the back of the group and pointed to the men. As the guilty men appeared out of the crowd, two burly policemen caught them.

'Right, you two,' said one. 'You are both under arrest for stealing that donkey.'

'Yes. That's the two who brought me the donkey foal,' shouted the salesman from the ring. 'That's them.'

As the policemen led the two thieves away, the salesman brought Nettie over to Skinny Man.

'Good job your goose made such a racket,' said the salesman, handing the harness rein to Skinny Man. 'This little lady might well have been sold; there was plenty of interest in her.'

'How did the police know about the thieves?' asked Mama Goose.

'I phoned them when I left you,' replied Skinny Man, 'and I phoned the farm. Mr and Mrs Farmer had just come home, and now Mr Farmer is coming to collect us.'

As they waited for Mr Farmer to come with his tractor and trailer, Skinny Man and Mama Goose made their way back to Bobby. When Mr Farmer arrived, he tethered Nettie safely into the attached container.

'We'll ride home on Bobby,' said Skinny Man, and so once more mounted on Bobby's back, Skinny Man and Mama Goose trotted back to the farm.

Mr Farmer and Mrs Farmer were delighted with Skinny Man, and with Mama Goose when they learned about her role in holding up the sales.

Three days later, Nettie's mum was back on the farm and fully recovered from her illness. She heard from Skinny Man about the adventures at the fair and thanked him and Mama Goose, and of course Bobby, for what they had done to rescue Nettie.

Later that day, a knock sounded on the farmhouse door. On the doorstep stood one of the two policemen who had arrested the thieves.

'Could I speak to the gentleman who called the station and helped catch those thieves?' the policeman asked.

'Certainly,' said Mr Farmer, and called for Skinny Man to come to the door.

'It appears,' the policeman explained, 'that those two were well known in another district, and had stolen and sold animals before.' He reached out an envelope to Skinny Man. 'It is a reward which was set up by another farmer for information leading to the capture of these thieves, and I reckon you deserve it.'

He opened the envelope. 'Wow!' he gasped. 'Twenty pounds!'

'Well done,' said Mr Farmer.

'Goodbye,' said the policeman.

'I think this money will go to buy something special for all the animals in my care,' said Skinny Man.

Later, he and Mama Goose related the whole story to the birds and animals on the farm, and they all looked forward to the something special that Skinny Man said he would provide.

So, that evening Mr Farmer and Mrs Farmer joined the animals and Skinny Man for a farmyard feast.

CHAPTER 2

Skinny Man and Mama Goose Go to the Seaside:

It was Skinny Man's day off, so he said to his friend Mama Goose, 'Today, we are taking a journey on a train.'

'A train!' exclaimed Mama Goose. 'I've never been on a train before; it sounds exciting. Where are we going?'

'Oh, that's a surprise,' answered Skinny Man, 'just wait and see.'

So off they went to the station and, when Skinny Man had bought their tickets, boarded the train. Because this was a market district, no-one seemed surprised to see a goose on the train. The two friends spent the morning on the beach, where Mama Goose was amazed when Skinny Man built sandcastles. Not only had Mama Goose never seen a sandcastle before, she had never been to the seaside before.

When he had finished at the beach, Skinny Man bought some lunch for himself and some exceptional food for Mama Goose. They were just finishing their lunch when they saw an open-topped bus coming down the prom. The driver was calling out, 'Stop me for a ride to the castle.'

Jumping down from their seat on the promenade, they boarded the bus and off they went to the castle.

The castle was bathed in sunlight when they arrived, but inside it was cold and dark. 'This way,' called the bus driver, who was now the tour guide. 'Follow me and keep close together.

Mama Goose, Skinny Man, and the other bus passengers followed the bus driver-guide into the castle courtyard. He told the story of the family who had owned the castle, and related the tragic tale of the young daughter who had fallen down the well.

He then told his audience, 'Some people say her ghost walks the corridors after dark, carrying a bucket of water.'

By the time the tour ended, the sun was going down and the party decided to leave the now darkening castle. But when they all arrived at the castle gate, it was locked.

'Is there no other way out?' asked one of the passengers.

'No,' replied their guide.

With that, the group made their way back to the castle and assembled in the large drawing-room. Skinny Man found a quiet corner for him and Mama Goose, but promptly fell asleep.

Mama Goose was bored and wandered off towards the corridors, where she hoped to see the ghost of the girl.

Ghosts, she thought to herself, *shouldn't frighten a goose.* But, although she waddled up and down and in and out of corridors and rooms, she saw no ghost. *I know*, she said to herself, *I'll look in the well.*

Outside went Mama Goose to search for the well. It took her a long time to find it, but to her astonishment, it was just inside the castle gate although slightly hidden by part of the wall.

Mama Goose peered down the well, but it was dark and she could see very little. So, opening her wings, she found she had just room enough to glide slowly down inside the shaft of the well.

The well seemed bottomless and very dark, but brave Mama Goose was not one bit frightened. Down, down she went, until finally she found herself sitting in water. There was no sign of any ghost, however, so Mama Goose decided that the ghost story was indeed only a story and not real.

Meanwhile, back in the castle, the bus driver had eventually managed to contact a key-keeper who very soon arrived and opened the castle gate.

'Sorry that you were locked in,' he said. 'The other keeper didn't see your bus and thought everyone had gone.'

'Now passengers,' called the driver, 'let's make our way to the bus.'

Skinny Man looked all around but couldn't see Mama Goose. *Perhaps she's already gone out*, he thought to himself, so he followed the other passengers to the bus. Just as the group walked through the courtyard, Mama Goose gently flapped her way up out of the well.

With shrieks of fright, the passengers watched in horror as this ghostly figure rose into the air. Except, that is, for Skinny Man who was too busy laughing because he recognised his feathered friend. Still shrieking, the passengers and the driver ran in terror out of the castle and raced around the corner to the parked bus.

Without checking that he had all his passengers aboard, the driver switched on the engine, put his coach in gear, and drove away at speed.

Mama Goose waddled over to Skinny Man. 'What just happened there?' she asked him.

'When you came up out of the well, they all thought you were the ghost,' Skinny Man said, still laughing. Mama Goose, in her funny goose laugh, soon joined in.

Just then the key-keeper approached Skinny Man and Mama Goose.

'What frightened them?' he asked.

When Skinny Man explained, the key-keeper also began to laugh.

Then Skinny Man said, 'But what about us? How will we get back to town? We need to catch a train in ten minutes.'

'Oh, don't worry,' said the key-keeper. 'My wife has flowers to take to the church, and she will transport you to the train station.'

He locked up the castle gate and took Skinny Man and Mama Goose back to his house.

'I wish your goose could come back for every bus tour. Once the story gets out, lots of folks will want to come and visit the castle, hoping for a glimpse of the mysterious ghost.'

'Afraid that wouldn't be possible,' said Skinny Man. 'We were only able to come because today was my day off.'

The key-keeper's wife arrived, and Skinny Man and Mama Goose climbed into her car. Soon they were at the station and, with a 'thank you' from Skinny Man, he and Mama Goose alighted. At the ticket desk, Skinny Man purchased tickets, and soon he and Mama Goose were on their way home.

'What a wonderful day,' said Skinny Man.

'A wonderful day indeed,' echoed Mama Goose, 'and a first- time seaside adventure for me.'

But, as once again Skinny Man and Mama Goose settled back into their lives on the farm, they secretly wondered, *What next?*

CHAPTER 3

Skinny Man and Mama Goose Go to America:

'Oh dear!' moaned Mama Goose. 'I do feel stiff.'

'When is the last time you flew any distance?' asked Skinny Man.

'I must admit, not for a long time,' Mama Goose replied.

'Right,' said Skinny Man, 'you are going flying!'

With that, he told Mama Goose to come with him and headed round the barn to Nettie's field. Nettie, the donkey foal, and her mum were pleased to see them.

'What brought about this visit?' asked Nettie.

'We are here because your field is just the place for this goose to start flying again,' Skinny Man replied.

With her big feet running across the grass, Mama Goose began her take-off run, then up she went into the air. Flap, flap went her wings, but she didn't get very far or very high. On landing, she just collapsed on her tummy feathers.

'Oh, I enjoyed that,' she said, quite out of breath, 'but I will need more practice.'

Once she got her breath back, Mama Goose and Skinny Man went back to the farmyard where they both went about their daily tasks.

'I tell you what,' said Skinny Man, 'I will put you on a diet.'

'What's all this about?' Mama Goose enquired. 'What is a diet? And why do I need to fly?'

Skinny Man produced a leaflet from his pocket. 'This leaflet says that in America they hold farmyard geese fly and swim races. Next month, Mr and Mrs Farmer are going to America on holiday. I thought that if I could get you ready in time, we could go too and enter the race.'

'You must be joking!' exclaimed Mama Goose. 'Go to America and race at my age - no way!' And with that, she waddled off to clean out her goose house.

Mr Farmer had discussed this possibility with Skinny Man and had asked him to persuade Mama Goose to join them on the trip. So, the next morning after completing his chores, Skinny Man again approached Mama Goose.

'What I didn't tell you yesterday is that Mr Farmer had the idea of the race and asked me to get you ready.'

'Well, actually,' responded Mama Goose, 'I kind of enjoyed my short flight yesterday and will try again today.'

'Right, 'said Skinny Man, 'to the field we go.' Round the barn and into the field they went, but this time Mama Goose led the way.

Nettie greeted them with a loud 'Hee haw' and trotted over to meet them.

'Are you going to try and fly again?' asked Nettie.

'Yes, and this time I am determined to stay in the air longer,' answered Mama Goose.

Once again, her feet went slap, slap across the grass until, with her wings flapping, Mama Goose rose up into the air. One minute, two minutes passed, and she covered quite a bit of distance before landing.

Skinny Man clapped his hands. 'Well done, my goose friend. If you keep this up, I can see you will win that race!' he shouted as he ran towards Mama Goose. 'Have a rest, and we will see how well you can swim.'

At the bottom of the next field was a large pond where the ducks swam every day. When she had rested, Mama Goose and Skinny Man headed to the duck pond. She had no problem paddling around twice before feeling tired. Climbing out, she said, 'I'm going to practise every day, because I want to go to America and win that fly and swim race.

'That's my girl,' said Skinny Man encouragingly, 'and tomorrow you will fly and swim again.' The weeks went quickly by, and each day Mama Goose kept to her diet even though she wasn't keen on the new food. With each passing day, she grew stronger, flew higher, and swam faster than the day before.

Geese in a nearby field looked up in amazement every day as Mama Goose flew by.

'I didn't know we geese could fly,' said one.

'We can't,' said another. 'That goose must be a stranger.' So, they just went on eating their grass and looking up at Mama Goose every day when she flew over their field.

Mr and Mrs Farmer had two sons, both married and living in America. Each year, having arranged for their neighbour to look after the farm, they would fly out to visit their families. This year was different, because now they had grandchildren to visit and they planned to travel by sea. Not far from the farm, there was a factory that made designer baby cots and beds, so Mr and Mrs Farmer bought two of each for their grandchildren.

On their last practice morning, Mama Goose and Skinny Man watched as a large van arrived to collect the furniture and the large cage for Mama Goose to live in during the voyage.

'I'm not too sure about living in a cage,' she said. But Skinny Man assured her that he had chosen it for her comfort. A short time later, when Mama Goose and Skinny Man arrived back at the farmyard, they saw the van driving off, taking everything to the ship.

Later that day, Skinny Man packed up his suitcase and a large box with everything Mama Goose would need for her journey and the race. And so, the following morning, a minibus arrived to collect Mr and Mrs Farmer, Skinny Man, and Mama Goose, to take them on the start of their journey to America. The cage containing Mama Goose, which turned out to be quite comfortable, was placed in a sheltered corner on deck.

The voyage began with the crossing of the vast Atlantic Ocean – next stop, America.

Mama Goose slept well the first night at sea. Next morning, Skinny Man awakened her. He opened the cage and out she stepped, only to be fitted with a collar and leash.

'What's this?' she asked, feeling quite alarmed. 'Why the collar?'

'It's rules,' explained Skinny Man. 'While at sea and on the deck, you need to wear a leash. It's what's called health and safety.'

'Oh well,' sighed Mama Goose, 'I suppose as I am not on the farm and at sea, I will have to walk with a collar on.'

Skinny Man and Mama Goose walked along the deck, Skinny Man holding onto the leash. They weren't alone on the ship's deck – others were there, some walking dogs. Folk all stared in amazement at Skinny Man and Mama Goose, who felt quite pleased at being the centre of attraction.

After several days had passed, Mama Goose stared in amazement to see a large lady standing on the water. Behind her was a city of huge buildings, some of which seemed to reach up to the sky. Skinny Man explained that the lady was a statue called 'The Statue of Liberty' and it was standing on a rock; the big city was New York.

'Mama Goose,' said Skinny Man, 'welcome to America!'

Once more back on dry land, Mr Farmer was now driving the van, with Mrs Farmer, Mama Goose, and Skinny Man on board, headed for their children's homes. On the way, Mr Farmer dropped Mama Goose and Skinny Man off at the race centre.

'We will join you tomorrow when we have left the furniture,' said Mr Farmer. 'Enjoy yourselves.'

A lady with a band on her arm which read 'Race Marshall', met Mama Goose and Skinny Man.

'Hello,' she greeted them, 'and welcome to the race centre. Let me show you to your cabin.'

The cage had remained in the van along with the collar and leash, so Mama Goose was free to walk with Skinny Man to their cabin. After a good night's rest, she felt terrific and ready for action.

Early that morning, the lady race marshal called to take them to the arena.

'Your goose will have two practice flights and swims which I will time,' she explained to Skinny Man. She then gave Skinny Man an armband to wear, with Mama Goose written on it.

'All the owners have to wear one with the name of their goose on it,' she explained.

Skinny Man was glad Mama Goose couldn't understand what she was saying, calling him her owner! This goose would have been very offended. The race marshal then gave Skinny Man a neckband with Mama Goose's name written on it.

'Each goose taking part in the race has to wear a collar,' she told him, 'just in case they get lost.'

Mama Goose was both excited and a little frightened when she saw the arena, but she and Skinny Man were not allowed to watch the other geese practising. When her turn came, Skinny Man followed the lady race marshal to the starting point.

Skinny Man had explained to Mama Goose what was about to happen. 'First, you will run downhill to a take-off point, where you will fly to the first pond. When you land on the water, you will see me in a small boat. I will direct you to swim between posts on the water and then to a long post, which is the water finish line. There, you and I will leave the water, run together up another hill to another take-off point. You will fly to the bottom of the hill, where the marshal will stop you by waving a flag, and she will check your time.'

It all happened just as Skinny Man said it would, and after her practice runs, Mama Goose was ready for her race.

This time they were able to watch the other geese start their first flight. Goose after goose took part in the race until, at last, it was the turn of Mama Goose. Feeling very nervous but ready to go, Mama Goose took off down the hill, into the air, and with a splash, into the water. Then as fast as she could, she swam between the markers pointed out by Skinny Man from his boat. Finally, out of the water and up the hill, she and Skinny Man ran.

Mama Goose ran as fast as she could down the short hill and into the air. With her wings flapping furiously, she flew to the finish line where Skinny Man waited.

'Well done,' said the marshal.

'That was great!' exclaimed a breathless Skinny Man to an even more breathless Mama Goose.

All the competitors gathered and waited for the results. The race marshal spoke into a microphone. First, she announced the name of the goose in third place; it wasn't Mama Goose.

Then she announced the name of the goose in second place; it wasn't Mama Goose.

Her head was beginning to sink, thinking she had not done well, when the race Marshall then announced, 'It gives me great pleasure to announce that the winner is...' – and there was a long pause – '...Mama Goose!'

Mr Farmer and Mrs Farmer, who had arrived at the arena in time to watch the race, came over very excitedly. Mrs Farmer hugged Mama Goose.

'Oh, you amazing and wonderful goose,' she said.

Mr Farmer shook Skinny Man by the hand and said, 'Well done'.

Skinny Man and Mama Goose walked up to the race marshal who presented Skinny Man with a large silver cup and an envelope containing the prize money of 100 dollars. All the spectators and competitors clapped their hands then waved as Skinny Man and Mama Goose left the arena.

Mr Farmer and Mrs Farmer were waiting in the van, and soon Skinny Man and Mama Goose were on their way home.

Mama Goose enjoyed the homeward journey. As she and Skinny Man walked around the deck each day, people stopped to talk, shake the hand of Skinny Man, and pat Mama Goose on the head. Everyone on board ship seemed to have heard of her success. She, of course, couldn't understand what folk were saying to Skinny Man, but afterwards when they were on their own, Skinny Man explained that the passengers and the ship's company had told him how thrilled and pleased they were to hear of Mama Goose's fantastic performance. Even the Captain stopped by to give his congratulations and to say that on the voyage, meals were free for Mr and Mrs Farmer, Skinny Man, and Mama Goose.

As the days went by, Mama Goose couldn't help but think and dream about her success. Soon the ship docked, and Mr and Mrs Farmer – in their van with Mama Goose and Skinny Man – were allowed to leave the vessel first. As they drove off, the passengers and crew waved goodbye.

Back home, a very excited Mama Goose rushed into the farmyard to tell all her friends about her fantastic win. Later, as Skinny Man settled her down for the night, he gave her one of his special goose treats for supper, patted her head, and went off to have his supper in the farmhouse. Proudly presented in the window was the silver cup, and once again Mr Farmer congratulated Skinny Man and said how proud he was of his special Mama Goose.

Another fantastic adventure was over for Mama Goose and Skinny Man; that is, until the next one!

CHAPTER 4

Skinny Man and Mama Goose Hunt for Treasure:

'Skinny Man,' called Mr Farmer. 'I need you to do a job for me in the house.'

'Right-o,' said Skinny Man, and followed Mr Farmer into the house. Mr Farmer and Skinny Man then climbed up two flights of stairs, went through a small door in the wall of one of the rooms, and into what Mr Farmer called the attic.

'As you can see, Skinny Man,' said Mr Farmer, pointing, 'the attic room is a bit of a mess, and I have no time to sort it out. See what you can do, and if you find anything that looks important put it aside for me to look at later.'

With that, Mr Farmer left him, and Skinny Man began looking through the stuff in the messy attic. He became so absorbed in his task that he didn't hear the attic door open, and got quite a shock when something in white appeared beside him. Startled, he looked round to find it was Mama Goose!

'I followed you and Mr Farmer into the house and hid in the kitchen until he left, then came upstairs to look for you,' explained Mama Goose. 'I didn't mean to startle you.'

'Here,' said Skinny Man, 'have a look at this.'

'You know I can't read human writing, what is it?' asked Mama Goose.

'It looks like an old map, and there is some writing on it. I'll need to clean it up before I can read it correctly,' Skinny Man replied, 'but now I had better get on with tidying up this attic. So, off you go before Mr Farmer misses you from the yard.'

Mama Goose was sad to leave the attic, but obediently she did as Skinny Man asked.

It took all morning for Skinny Man to sort out what was essential and what was junk, but finally, he had finished. He took the important stuff to Mr Farmer but kept the dirty map in his pocket until he could read it.

Skinny Man then put together a food basket for himself and Mama Goose and went to find her.

'Mama Goose,' he called, and when she answered, he said, 'I have brought our lunch and some cloths to clean the old map.'

So, off they both went for their lunch, and afterwards, Skinny Man began very carefully to clean the map. Slowly but surely pictures and writing appeared until Skinny Man, very excitedly, exclaimed, 'Mama Goose, this is a treasure map.'

Mama Goose, of course, had no idea what a map was, never mind a treasure map, so she just looked on as Skinny Man began to read.

This map is a guide to a treasure that was buried by pirates many years ago at Riddlington Hill. I have searched the caves there many times trying to find it, but now I am too old to look any more. I will tell my son about this map so he can continue the search.

Signed, Grandfather Farmer

'I'd better show this to Mister Farmer,' said Skinny Man, and off he went to look for him. When he found Mr Farmer, he showed him the map.

'Well, I don't know anything about this!' exclaimed a surprised Mr Farmer. 'This is my father's father who wrote this, my grandfather. My father never mentioned this to me; perhaps he never found the map. Skinny man,' he added, 'this is fascinating, but I have no time to look for treasure. If I give you time off work to search, will you do so?' he asked.

'Delighted to help out,' said Skinny Man, 'and do you mind if I take Mama Goose with me?'

'Why on earth would you want to take the goose?' asked Mr Farmer. 'You took her with you to the seaside as well. How strange.'

Of course, Mr Farmer didn't know that Skinny Man and Mama Goose were friends who could talk to each other.

'Yes, take her along,' said Mr Farmer as he walked away, shaking his head. *What a strange young man*, he said to himself.

There was certainly something different about a person who could talk to animals, but Skinny Man was born that way.

Skinny Man went to the storehouse and found an old metal detector. He found and placed three batteries inside the battery compartment. When Skinny Man switched the metal detector on, it worked, making a loud buzzing noise as it passed over some nails. He also found a torch which he decided would be useful in dark caves.

'What was that noise?' asked Mama Goose, appearing at the storehouse door.

'That,' said Skinny Man, 'is called a metal detector, and as treasure is metal, it will help us find it. Mr Farmer's grandfather wouldn't have had one of these, but I knew Mr Farmer had one.'

So, with a packed basket of food, the metal detector, and torch, Skinny Man and Mama Goose set off for Riddlington Hill caves.

It was a long walk to the caves, and at times Skinny Man had to carry Mama Goose. It was almost dark by the time they reached the caves, so they found a sheltered spot and, after supper, settled down for the night.

Next morning after breakfast, the two friends headed into the cave. They hadn't gone far when they saw something partially buried in the sandy floor of the cave. When the Skinny Man lifted it out and switched on his torch, he could see it was a piece of paper with a drawing of a pirate's flag and, in big letters, the words: TREASURE HUNTERS BEWARE OF CAPTAIN JAKE.

'What does it say?' asked Mama Goose.

So Skinny Man told her. 'But I'm not sure what it means, or who Captain Jake is,' he added.

'Well, never mind,' said Mama Goose, 'let's get on with our exciting treasure hunt.'

Shining his torch, Skinny Man led Mama Goose deeper into the cave. He also switched on the metal detector, and as they walked, Skinny Man waved it to and fro over the ground.

They both got excited when it made its buzzing noise, only to find it was a tin can buried in the sand. After two more disappointments like this, they moved deeper into the cave – but nothing!

Skinny Man and Mama Goose made their way back to where they had slept the night before and ate some lunch.

'After lunch, we will try another cave,' said Skinny Man.

Not far inside the second cave, they again found a note just like the first one, with the same warning.

'To pot with Captain Jake whoever he is, we will keep on looking,' said Skinny Man, 'but I wish the map showed us in which cave we would find the treasure.'

Again, using the metal detector, Skinny Man, followed by Mama Goose, walked into the cave and found... more tin cans.

There was no sign of any treasure, so Skinny Man and Mama Goose went back to have supper. 'We will look in the last cave tomorrow, but now I am so tired,' said Skinny Man.

'Me too,' said Mama Goose. And as soon as they had eaten their supper, they both fell fast asleep.

During the night, Skinny Man was wakened by something sharp digging into his ribs.

Oh! he thought, still half asleep. *It's Captain Jake with his pirate sword!* But no, it was Mama Goose with her sharp beak.

'Wake up,' she whispered, 'there is someone in the cave.'

At once, Skinny Man was wide awake. 'Listen,' Mama Goose said, still whispering, 'I can hear voices.'

Skinny Man listened, but all he could hear was the wind gently whistling through the cave. 'Go back to sleep, Mama Goose,' he said, 'you are letting your imagination get the better of you.'

Next morning when Skinny Man woke, he saw writing on the sandy cave floor, close to where he was sleeping.

Last warning, treasure hunter. Go home.

'I knew it!' exclaimed a frightened Mama Goose. 'Captain Jake doesn't want us to find his treasure!'

'Calm down, Mama Goose,' said Skinny Man. 'Ghostly pirates from the past don't write like that. But someone doesn't want us snooping around here. Come on, eat your breakfast, then we are going back to the cave. You must have slept well in your corner not to hear or see anything or anyone.'

'I wasn't in the cave all night,' said Mama Goose. 'After hearing those voices, I went into the dunes to sleep, I only came back into the cave as you were waking up. And I think I will stay in the dunes; I've had enough treasure hunting. I will keep watch for anyone coming.'

'Right you are,' laughed Skinny Man. 'If I come across Captain Jake, I will call out "Don't harm me, Captain Jake", and you can come to my rescue.'

Still laughing softly to himself, Skinny Man headed into the last cave with torch, map, and metal detector; off to the dunes to keep watch went Mama Goose.

Unfortunately, Mama Goose and Skinny Man did not know that the third cave had a rear entrance from the other side of the dunes. As Skinny Man went further into the cave, he came upon many boxes.

'These don't look like treasure chests,' he murmured to himself as he opened one of the boxes. Inside were bottles of perfume and other packages and containers. Skinny Man immediately knew what these were. They were items smuggled in from a foreign land for sale in this country.

He opened another box and found bags of animal feed with international writing on the packages. 'Oh dear,' said Skinny

Man, this time out loud. 'If I fed any animal this stuff, it might harm them. I will have to go and phone the police.'

'Oh no, me hearty, you won't be going anywhere,' said what sounded like a pirate voice.

As Skinny Man turned around, he saw two pirates coming towards him. And before he could do or say anything, they jumped on him and knocked him to the ground.

While all this was going on, Mama Goose felt hungry and was trying to eat the coarse dune grass. As she tugged at a clump of grass, it came away, dragging something else with it. Poking her beak into the bunch of grass, she pulled, and suddenly a large piece of cloth came away. Mama Goose fell backwards, and she and the fabric went rolling down the dune.

As she struggled to free herself, she heard Skinny Man shout, 'Don't harm me, Captain Jake!'

Knowing her friend was in trouble, and unable to get untangled from the cloth, Mama Goose spread her wings and flew towards the cave.

Inside the cave, the pirates laughed. 'Ha, ha, do you think one of us is Captain Jake?' said one. 'There is no Captain Jake; we made him up to frighten you,' said the other pirate.

'Oh, then,' exclaimed Skinny Man, pointing, 'this must be Captain Jake.'

Hearing a whirring sound, the two pirates turned around to see a towering black figure zooming into the cave. In their panic, they turned to run but, stretching out his long legs, Skinny Man tripped them both. They crashed to the floor, knocking their heads on the rocks protruding from the sand.

By this time, Mama Goose had managed to untangle herself from most of the black cloth, and watched as Skinny Man took some rope from the boxes and began to tie the two pirates up. With her beak, Mama Goose pulled at the pirates' strange-looking faces, and masks came away.

'Well, well,' said Skinny Man, 'I've seen these two before. They live in the village close to our farm.'

He knew now that these men were the smugglers and that he would have to fetch the police. Reaching out, he helped Mama Goose get untangled from the rest of the black cloth, then switched on his torch for a closer look.

'Mama Goose,' he asked, 'where did you find this?'

Mama Goose explained about the clump of grass on the dune.

'This, Mama Goose, is a pirate flag,' said Skinny Man. 'Show me where you found it.'

Leaving the two smugglers tied up in the cave, Skinny Man gathered up his metal detector and torch and followed Mama Goose to where she had found the flag. As they approached the spot, suddenly the metal detector, which Skinny Man had forgotten to switch off, began to buzz. Skinny Man waved the metal detector over the area where Mama Goose had found the flag, and the buzz grew louder.

He switched off the metal detector and began to dig in the sand with his hands. Soon Mama Goose joined in, using her webbed feet. Before long, the top of a box appeared. But as they dug further, Skinny Man found it was not a box but a chest.

With the help of Mama Goose, he was able to drag the casket out of the hole they had dug in the sand. The lock on the chest was old, and as Skinny Man struck it with his torch, it opened and fell off.

When Skinny Man opened the chest, he discovered that it was not just a chest but a treasure chest, filled with jewels and gold coins.

'Wow'! exclaimed Skinny Man. 'We've found the pirate's treasure.' He closed the lid and said, 'Right, Mama Goose, here's what we do. You stay with the treasure chest, and I will run as fast as I can back to the farm and fetch Mr Farmer.'

So, off went Skinny Man, running over the sand and onto the road then on towards the farm. Mama Goose made herself as comfortable as she could, sitting on top of the treasure chest.

When Skinny Man reached the farm, he breathlessly told Mr Farmer all that had happened at Riddlington Hill caves. Mr Farmer phoned the police and informed them about the smugglers and where they would find them, then he hitched Bobby the farm horse to his cart and briskly they trotted back to the sand dunes.

When they arrived, they could see Mama Goose on the top of the sand dune. Mr Farmer and Skinny Man climbed to where she was, and then Mr Farmer saw the treasure chest. Mama Goose jumped down, and Skinny Man opened it.

Mr Farmer's eyes nearly popped out of his head when he saw what was inside the chest. 'My word, my word,' was all he could say.

'So,' said Skinny Man, 'what do we do now?'

Just then, they saw the police arrive and take the two smugglers in handcuffs to the police wagon. The smuggled goods were carried out, and a police van drove over the sand to collect them.

'Now,' said Mr Farmer, 'let's get this chest down to the cart.'

Pushing, pulling, lifting, and shoving it, they managed to bring the chest down the dune and into the cart. Mr Farmer, Skinny Man, and Mama Goose climbed aboard, and Bobby, again with a brisk trot, soon had them back at the farm.

'What will happen to the treasure?' asked Skinny Man.

'Well, it is called "treasure trove" and belongs to the government, but I'm sure there will be a reward,' explained Mr Farmer, as he and Skinny Man lifted the treasure chest from the cart and carried it into the farmhouse.

Mr Farmer then released Bobby from the cart, and Skinny Man led the big horse to the stable for some well-earned refreshment and a rub-down.

Sure, enough, the government were delighted to receive the treasure trove.

'We were never sure if this existed,' said the important government officer, 'and all these years, treasure hunters have been looking in the wrong place.'

Shaking the hands of Mr Farmer and Skinny Man, the government person added, 'Oh, by the way, there will be a reward.'

Of course, only Skinny Man knew of the vital part Mama Goose had played in the discovery. Later, she and Skinny Man laughed and laughed as he told her again and again how she had frightened those pirate fellows when she swooped into the cave with the pirate flag wrapped around her.

CHAPTER 5

Mama Goose's Magic Moment:

Mama Goose came out of her goose house just as Skinny Man led a newly brushed and mane-combed Bobby, the farm horse, into the yard.

'Oh!' exclaimed Mama Goose. 'Where is Bobby going?'

'To the fair,' answered Skinny Man. 'He is taking part in the horse show.'

'I didn't know Bobby could jump,' said Mama Goose.

'Not showjumping, Mama Goose,' laughed Skinny Man. 'Bobby is in the "best looking carthorse" competition.'

With that, Skinny Man led Bobby into a horsebox and put a bag containing grain over his face and head. He then attached the horsebox to Mr Farmer's tractor.

'Come on, Mama Goose,' called Skinny Man, 'you don't want to miss this.' He then told Mama Goose everything that would take place at the fair. 'There will be all kinds of food stalls and fairground attractions to see.'

Mama Goose had no idea about fairground attractions, but it all sounded exciting, so she waddled into the horsebox to ride with Bobby.

Mr Farmer arrived in the yard and told Skinny Man to drive the tractor to the fair. He then added, 'I'll follow behind with Mrs Farmer in our car.'

Off they went, with Skinny Man driving the tractor and towing the horsebox with Mama Goose and Bobby inside, and Mr and Mrs Farmer following behind.

Mama Goose was very excited. She had never been to this kind of fair before and asked Bobby, 'Bobby, what are fairground attractions?'

But Bobby was too busy munching at the grain in his nosebag to answer.

After what seemed to Mama Goose like a very long journey, the tractor stooped moving and then Skinny Man opened the back door of the horsebox and laid it on the ground as a ramp. Out waddled Mama Goose, then Skinny Man backed Bobby out, minus his nosebag, and started brushing him again.

Mr Farmer appeared and patted Bobby. 'You are looking well, my friend,' he said. 'Now off we go to the horse paddock.'

Mama Goose had seen horse paddocks before, and so she pecked at Skinny Man's trousers to get his attention. 'Where are the fairground attractions?' she asked.

'Oh,' answered Skinny Man, 'they don't start up till after the horse show finishes. But come on, let's look at the stalls.'

A very bored Mama Goose followed Skinny Man as he looked at some stalls and bought a few things, but she perked up when he purchased some items at the food stall for her to eat.

The loudspeakers announced the horse show, so Skinny Man and Mama Goose made their way to the arena to see if Bobby would win a prize. Several horses were paraded before the judges before it was Bobby's turn. The Judges looked him up and down, checking his hooves, legs, and teeth, and making notes on their clipboard paper.

Soon it was time to announce the winner. Bobby didn't win, but he came second and received a red rosette and ribbon.

Mr Farmer seemed delighted at the result and told Skinny Man, 'I expected that horse to win, but for Bobby to come second was a wonderful surprise, as this was his first time to take part in a horse show.'

He shook Skinny Man by the hand and said, 'Well done, and Bobby looked splendid today.'

He then handed Skinny Man the keys to his car and said, 'Mrs Farmer has met up with some friends and is staying on for a while. I'll take Bobby back, and you can bring Mrs Farmer home later in the car,'

All over the fairground, lights came on.

Skinny Man said, 'Looks like the fairground attractions are about to start.'

The first attraction they stopped at was what is known as a Coconut Shy. Here the Skinny Man paid 5p and was given three hard balls. At the back of the stall was a row of small poles with cups on top. Each one contained a coconut. The idea was to knock a coconut off the pole, but although Skinny Man threw as hard as he could, and indeed hit one coconut, none fell to the ground.

The next attraction was a shooting gallery where Mama Goose watched as Skinny Man tried to shoot one or more of the wooden ducks which were moving along a rail. This time, Skinny Man shot down five of the eight ducks and won a prize: a small teddy bear.

The next attraction had a showman with a big moustache, wearing a top hat and standing on a platform, who was calling for someone to volunteer to step into a large cabinet.

'No-one will come to any harm, I assure you,' he shouted. 'You will disappear for a few minutes, and I will make you reappear in the other cabinet.' He pointed to a second cabinet at the other end of the platform. 'Whoever volunteers will receive a prize.' And he pointed to a table with lots of items displayed on it.

'Sir,' he called to Skinny Man, 'why not let your goose be a volunteer? I promise you, she will be fine.'

Mama Goose was not too confident, but she did like an adventure so, in goose talk which only Skinny Man could understand, she agreed. Skinny Man handed Mama Goose to the showman who placed her into one of two cabinets. He then closed the door and muttered what Skinny Man supposed were some magic words.

A bright flash and large puff of smoke came up from the floor of the platform in front of the cabinet, and when the showman opened the cabinet door, Mama Goose had vanished. He then walked over and opened the second cabinet, and there was Mama Goose, looking bewildered (although only Skinny Man could read the expression on her face) but unharmed.

The watching crowd and Skinny Man clapped their hands at this fantastic piece of magic. The showman handed Mama Goose to Skinny Man, along with another prize – this time a small clock.

When Skinny Man asked Mama Goose what had happened, she said she didn't know. She told him that she seemed to fall asleep and was surprised to come out of the other cabinet.

As Skinny Man and Mama Goose walked away, a man approached them who said that he worked for the magician and asked if they could use the goose at a later show.

'That depends on how late,' said Skinny Man. 'We have to go home once we have had something to eat.'

'The next show is in an hour, if that would suit,' replied the magician's helper.

Just then, Skinny Man spied Mrs Farmer and her friends. 'Let me check with my boss,' he said, and he and Mama Goose approached Mrs Farmer.

'Hello,' said Mrs Farmer, 'I hope you are not ready to go home yet.'

'No,' replied Skinny Man, then he told her about the show.

'Oh!' exclaimed Mrs Farmer. 'I would like to see that. I will meet you at the magician's stall in an hour.' And she went off with her friends to have some tea.

'I think we will get something to eat, too,' said Skinny Man to Mama Goose. 'Let's go to the vegetable stall and buy something for you.'

When they had both eaten – some lettuce for Mama Goose, and a meat pie from the pie stall for Skinny Man – they headed back to the magician's booth.

Mrs Farmer and her friends were already there, and when the magician saw Skinny Man, he called out, 'Ah! Here comes my assistant Mrs Goose and her friend.'

When it was her turn to perform, Skinny Man lifted Mama Goose onto the platform. The magician explained what was about to happen then placed Mama Goose into the first cabinet.

Once again, after some muttered magic words, came the flash and smoke. When the magician opened the cabinet, as before, Mama Goose had vanished. The showman then walked across the platform to the other one and opened it, but this time there was no Mama Goose!

'I don't understand,' said the showman, 'the goose should have been here.'

Skinny Man leapt onto the platform and searched inside and behind the cabinets, but there was no sign of Mama Goose.

Mrs Farmer shouted at the showman, 'Where is my goose? This goose is exceptional.'

'I'm sorry,' said the showman, 'this has never happened before. I will make inquires with my assistants.'

'It was one of your assistants who asked us to come back for the second show,' said Skinny Man to the showman, 'but I don't see him about.'

'I didn't ask for you to come back,' cried the showman. 'I had someone else lined up for the second show, but when I saw the goose, I thought I would use her again. I did not send an assistant to ask you to come back.'

Just then, one of the fairground policemen arrived, summoned by Mrs Farmer. When it was explained to him what had happened, he blew into his whistle and two more policemen arrived.

'Right,' instructed the first policeman, 'we are looking for a thief with a stolen white goose.' Then, turning to the showman, he asked how this could happen.

'I shouldn't give away my secrets, but this is how it happens.' The showman whispered into the policeman's ear the secrets of the trick so that no-one else could hear.

'Right,' said the policeman, turning to Skinny Man. 'what did this so-called assistant look like?'

Skinny Man was able to give a good description of the man. Overhearing the conversation, the showman exclaimed, 'I know that man! He used to work for me, but I had to dismiss him for stealing some of the prizes. He has some friends who still work at the fair. I will take you to where they are.'

The showman set off, followed by the policemen, Skinny Man, and Mrs Farmer. After a while, Skinny Man said, 'Stop! I can hear Mama Goose calling my name.'

'Calling your name!' exclaimed the first policeman. 'I don't understand. How can you hear a goose call your name?'

'Never mind that,' said Skinny Man, 'follow me.'

What the others didn't know was that Mama Goose could squeal in a high-pitched call that no-one could hear except her friend Skinny Man. The group followed him to a hut at the side of the fairground.

'Stay here,' instructed the first policeman, then he and the other officer kicked open the shed door and rushed inside. There were shouts and the sound of a scuffle, and then out came the first policeman carrying Mama Goose, followed by the other policeman holding firmly onto two men.

'That's the one,' said Skinny Man pointing to the thief. 'That's the one who said he was your assistant.'

Mama Goose jumped down from the arms of the first policeman, and Mrs Farmer stooped down and hugged her tightly. 'Oh, I am so glad you are safe,' she cried.

As Skinny Man walked away, followed by Mama Goose and Mrs Farmer, the policeman wanted to know how he could hear a goose calling his name.

'I can't tell you,' said Skinny Man, 'it's a secret.'

The showman continued to follow Skinny Man.

'Sir,' he said, 'I would pay you handsomely to come and work with me. I could use you and the goose in my act.'

'Sorry,' said Skinny Man. 'Firstly, the goose does not belong to me, and secondly, Mama Goose and I have better things to do.'

'Don't you want to press charges?' asked the first policeman.

'No,' said Skinny Man, 'I'll leave that to the showman.'

'Now,' said Mrs Farmer as they walked towards the car, 'you must tell me how you can hear a goose call your name.'

'If I told you,' laughed Skinny Man, 'I would have to shoot you.'

'Oh, you!' exclaimed Mrs Farmer, laughing and gently punching him on his shoulder. 'You can keep your secret.'

They all laughed as they climbed into the car, but only Skinny Man could hear Mama Goose.

Lightning Source UK Ltd.
Milton Keynes UK
UKHW010647120720
366375UK00001B/14

9 781839 751370